Rose's Promise

Cindy,
Happy reading!
Karen Hoelsker Johnson

Rose's Promise

Karen Hoelscher Johnson

TATE PUBLISHING
AND ENTERPRISES, LLC

Rose's Promise
Copyright © 2015 by Karen Hoelscher Johnson. All rights reserved.

No part of this publication may be reproduced, stored in a retrieval system or transmitted in any way by any means, electronic, mechanical, photocopy, recording or otherwise without the prior permission of the author except as provided by USA copyright law.

This novel is a work of fiction. Names, descriptions, entities, and incidents included in the story are products of the author's imagination. Any resemblance to actual persons, events, and entities is entirely coincidental.

The opinions expressed by the author are not necessarily those of Tate Publishing, LLC.

Published by Tate Publishing & Enterprises, LLC
127 E. Trade Center Terrace | Mustang, Oklahoma 73064 USA
1.888.361.9473 | www.tatepublishing.com

Tate Publishing is committed to excellence in the publishing industry. The company reflects the philosophy established by the founders, based on Psalm 68:11,
"The Lord gave the word and great was the company of those who published it."

Book design copyright © 2015 by Tate Publishing, LLC. All rights reserved.
Cover design by Samson Lim
Interior design by Shieldon Alcasid

Published in the United States of America

ISBN: 978-1-68164-007-5
1. Fiction / Christian / Historical
2. Fiction / Family Life
15.07.10

This book is dedicated to the following persons who have encouraged me along the way:

Charles, my husband, has shown infinite patience from the time of my first book to this sequel. Our four daughters—Emily, Erica, Erin, and Elisha—have encouraged and straightened out computer problems during the writing of this book. Also, much love to our four beautiful grandchildren—Eden, Isaaq, Atira, and Ellison—who are our pride and joy.

Introduction

THE PASTEL DRAWING used for the cover of this story—a sequel to *Lancaster's Rose*—was drawn by my great-aunt Carrie Duden. She grew up on a farm south of the little town of Williams, Iowa. She was an excellent artist. Lured off the farm with hopes of an easier life in the city, Carrie found work in a drugstore in Des Moines, Iowa. At the age of eighteen, she died in childbirth. The year was 1909. The house in which Carrie and several of her siblings were born, including my grandfather, burned to the ground in the 1930s. The house was rebuilt, and my mother was born there. The land is now farmed by my brother Lurlin.

Chapter 1

Jed woke up to the sun shining brightly in the window. The events of the day before flooded back to his mind, and he was afraid to turn over to see if Rose was really there. He lay there only a moment before cautiously turning over to gaze at the woman beside him. Rose was still sleeping, gently breathing as she slumbered. Almost unable to believe that she was there with him, he thought back to yesterday remembering the events of that wonderful afternoon. Finally, after nearly two years of trying to forget her, there she was on the stagecoach coming back to Lancaster to join Jed on the farm. Thinking that she was one of the women answering his request for a mail-order bride, he was embarrassed to have the entire town watching him meet the stage. Instead of a stranger exiting the stage, out stepped the beautiful auburn-haired woman who had been forced to travel back East with her parents and baby sister in search of a cure for her ailing father. After losing her father and caring for her mother who suffered a stroke soon afterward, Rose gave up hope that she would ever be able to return to Lancaster and the man she loved. Caring for her baby sister and repaying medical bills for both parents kept Rose living in the East. Rose and Hope's mother died within a year and with the help of Jed's parents, unbeknown to Jed, Rose and Hope came on the stage to be with Jed.

Those were some of the setbacks that occurred before Rose and Hope could start out for Iowa. They had to wait until the weather turned a bit warmer. Rose was anxious to start out earlier, but Hope was too young to endure the changing, sometimes hostile weather that the spring often brought. The pair traveled three hundred miles of terrain that changed from one day to the next. When there was a dry spell, the roads were dusty. However, with the rains that this time of year brought, there were often muddy ruts in the roads and the driver had to dig the wheels out. The bumps of the unforgiving roads were barely noticed by Rose as she pondered over whether she had made a sensible decision to leave the city for a life in the West. She held a beautiful toddler in her lap the entire way—a little girl who had very similar features to her older sister. Auburn curls that framed her heart-shaped face fell across it as the wind blew in from the windows.

But the scenery was beautiful. Apple blossoms were beginning to come out in full force. The green grass was taking over the brown grass that had been left behind with the coming of spring. Frogs were full-throated as they were trying to make themselves known to prospective mates. Nature was waking up as they traveled westward. Squirrels hustled here and there, digging for their hidden stashes, trying to make them last until the new crop of nuts appeared. Hope clapped with delight when she saw a fawn or two with mothers searching and nibbling for the grass that the new season offered. Creeks and little brooks were running quickly, and the rocks that had been covered with snow now had a glossy shine from having water run over them once again. When the driver pulled by the water sources so the horses could quench their thirst, Rose led Hope to some of the birds nests that were located on the lower branches. She lifted Hope up so that she might see the eggs that the nearby scolding mother bird was protecting.

Most nights brought a new location to stay. Several nights, the stage stopped by the side of the road because they hadn't been able to make it to the next town because of the conditions of the road. On those nights, Rose and Hope slept in the coach with a board for a mattress and a blanket of sorts with which to cover. The next morning, Rose would wake up stiff and sore. The sleeping conditions didn't seem to bother Hope. Some of the overnight stops were rough and isolated, but Rose and Hope were treated kindly.

They waited for nearly three days before they could be ferried across the Mississippi River into Iowa. Flooding had made the crossing treacherous, so there was nothing to do but wait. They were invited to stay at the local church's parsonage as their guests. It was a relief for Rose to let Hope have a chance to run around and play with the parson's small children. It was good to hear her sweet laughter as she played games with the children and the family's dog. Her peals of joy could be heard as the friendly little dog licked Hope's face. When they were able to travel again, it was difficult to say good-bye to the people who had treated them so kindly. For three days, the girls enjoyed not being in the jolting stage. The wooden seats were unforgiving as they were jostled around on the unpredictable roads.

Sometimes, there were others in the stage with them. They met a young doctor who was on his way to set up a practice in central Iowa. He appeared to be interested in Rose but not in Hope.

"I am looking for a nurse to help me in my practice. I could train you to learn what you needed to know."

"Thank you, but I am heading to Lancaster, Iowa. I am going to be a farm wife."

"What kind of a life will that be? Working hard for nothing."

"I don't think that at all. We have our farm and each other. It will be a good life."

"Then you must be terribly naïve."

"I have my sister to think of. Growing up in a city would not be the kind of life I want for her."

"She'll always be a burden. You should put her in an orphanage and get on with your life."

Rose glared at the man, feeling quite annoyed with him and his suggestions.

Several miles down the road, the stage stopped at a water trough in a small town. The young doctor stepped out of the coach and turned to Rose. "Tell the driver that I am getting a refreshment to drink at the saloon. I'll be back in about ten or fifteen minutes."

Within a couple of minutes, the driver came and peered in the stage. "Where's the doctor?"

Rose thought only a moment before responding. "He decided to get out here and said to throw down his bag and leave without him."

"Okay, little lady." With that he climbed to his seat in front of the coach, threw off the doctor's bag, and picked up the reins. Leaving the town with a small cloud of dust, the stage headed off toward the day's destination. Rose smiled thinking about the arrogant man that had been left behind.

It wasn't long before a young woman who was going to set up a dress-and-hat shop joined Rose and Hope in the stage. She delighted Rose by sharing with her some of the new styles in women's clothing. Holding a ladies' magazine between them, many miles passed by as the two, with heads close together, peered over the pattern styles that graced the pages.

"Here, this one has a larger bustle in the back. The petticoats help the dress to flair out and cover the model's shoes."

"How beautiful the lace is!" exclaimed Rose. "The beadwork is exquisite! How can something such as that be so cheaply priced?"

"These dresses are made by a sewing machine. I have one in my crates on the top rack."

"Aren't they expensive?"

"Yes, but it pays for itself with the sewing of ten dresses. Even the best of the seamstress couldn't possibly equal the small stitches that the machine makes."

"I suppose that I'll never own one," Rose lamented. "It wouldn't make sense for one woman to own one."

Several afternoons later, the young woman had reached her destination, and they bid each other a fond farewell.

It was interesting to have someone else to visit with, and she did miss the companionship of the young seamstress, but Rose preferred to just to sit and to think. She enjoyed the times she and Hope were alone. When there was no other passengers, Rose would let Hope sit on the benches, but when Hope slept, Rose would hold her as the bumps of the road would wake her up from her naps.

The spring weather made most of the trip quite pleasant. There were a few days of rain and thunderstorms that shook the coach so terribly that the driver was forced to seek protection in a farmer's barn.

"Sorry, lil' miss. But we'll have to take shelter in the barn. With a storm like this, we'll get blown off the road. Might as well try to catch some shut-eye. We'll get going as soon as we are able."

So Rose doze on and off, while Hope had a more restful sleep. She had a few interruptions. As she was slowly getting comfortable, Rose felt something tickling her bare feet. Sitting straight up, she peered in the dark and threw a wayward hen, which was looking for a dry spot for her nest, out of the stage back into the barn. As the storm pounded the wooden structure Rose thought about what the doctor said. Was she naïve for thinking that she and Jed could make a good living on the farm? She looked fondly at Hope. Keeping Hope was the easiest of all the decisions that she had to make. They were bonded together for life by the blood that they shared. She would tell Hope about their parents and how wonderful they were and how much they loved their girls. In remembrance, Rose wiped away tears.

As they traveled West, Rose watched the wildlife and enjoyed pointing all of the different animals that she and Hope saw along the way. She wondered why she hadn't seen many buffalo and asked the driver about it when they stopped to rest the horses one afternoon.

"Well," he replied, "the railroads have hired sharpshooters to kill them as they damage the tracks and so forth. They get paid a bounty on each one that they kill."

"That sounds terrible!" exclaimed Rose.

"Yes, ma'am. It also forced the Indians to live in other places because those animals were one thing they needed to live out here on the plains. They used every part of the bison for food, shelter, and even their tools. It is a waste."

"The poor Indians. Where did they go?"

"Farther West. But they were mad and rightfully so. For a time, settlers had difficulties with them and got themselves shot. But then the government showed up and forced them to other places."

"What about the other animals that used the buffalo for food? What are they doing for food?"

"The wolves pretty much moved on. Only a few of the older ones and mothers with pups stayed behind. The problem now that this area faces is the drought. It seems to have localized in the central strip of Iowa."

Rose thought about this often and thought how sad that the country was changing so.

Finally came the sunny afternoon when the sights along the trail became familiar to Rose. Good memories of Jed and his family filled her mind as she passed spots that held meanings for her. Looking in the distance, she could see Jed's parents' home. Jenny and Benjamin had been instrumental in helping Rose come back to Lancaster. Peering ahead, she could see the roof of the school where she had first met Jed. It was the night of the school expedition, and remembering when their eyes first meet, her face flushed red. That was also where they went to singing school together and became a couple. She could see the top of the general store that her aunt and uncle used to own. When Rose's father was not able to meet his brother out West, her aunt and uncle decided to go to be part of a new adventure. They packed up nearly everything that they had in their store to use for supplies and headed out to the Dakotas. When they left, Lancaster was without a store for a couple of months but was soon back in business with new owners. Her grandparents had also died, so Rose was coming back to a place that no longer had any family, but there was even something more important that she was interested in, and that was Jed. On the small knoll stood the little white church that Rose and Jed would have been married in. She wondered if Parson Jones was still around or if he was in another town, annoying those townspeople with his sermons.

Even though she had been gone for nearly two years, her love for Jed was as strong as it had ever been. She hoped that it was the same feeling he had for her.

As the wagon wheels rolled closer to Lancaster, she could see the hustle and bustle of the town's activity. She had actually been a part of Lancaster for such a short time she wondered why it felt so much like home.

There certainly seemed to be a lot of people milling about in town. Nearing the general store, the driver pulled the reins of the team so abruptly that Rose's hat fell over her face. For this she was grateful. She could peek out from under the rim of the hat and search the terrain. She spotted Jed who appeared a trite bit indifferent. But she was sure that she had never seen a more handsome man as her heart jumped and her stomach felt as if there were butterflies in it. She forced herself to be patient and waited until the driver threw the bag down to Jed before helping Hope from the stage. She could see his reaction to the baby and chuckled to herself while thinking of how he must feel that moment and not knowing that she was here. She backed down the coach's steps and did not put her hat high upon her head until she was sure Jed was in front of her.

As she lifted her head, his reaction was greater than she expected. Any doubts of how he felt about her quickly vanished, and he embraced her so tightly she couldn't breathe.

"Your parents kept my secret, didn't they?"

"I never thought I would see you again, and now here you are! You are more beautiful than I remember!" Having said this, he looked into the stage then at Rose with questioning eyes.

She knew what he was asking without saying a word. "Mama died about nine months ago. It took that long to figure out what to do and how to do it."

"Rose, why didn't you let me know? I would have helped somehow."

"Your mother wired me the money to come out on the stage. So here we are, Hope and I. Do you think we could have that life that we wanted on our little farm? Hope has to be a part of it."

His smile was his reply as he swept up Rose and twirled around with her. For a moment, it was as if they were the only two people in Lancaster. It looked as if there would be a wedding. Already the women of the church were heading up to the church with their arms full of the spring flowers. The men in the shops tried to appear uninterested, but all eyes were upon the young couple as they were reunited. Several women dabbed at eyes that were misted over. Not one of them didn't wish for her husband to display open affection, and a few secretly vowed to rekindle her husband's devotions. It was rare to see a young couple, or even an older couple, publicly show their love for one another. It did a lot of hearts good to see two young people so much in love. Too often, hard work pushed feelings to the back of the mind, and too many reasoned that was what the pioneer life was like—all work and very little time for pleasure.

Jed offered his arm to the lovely woman who had just exited the stage, and with her accepting it, they began to walk. As they strolled up to the church arm in arm, Rose whispered, "Jed, why are there so many people here?"

"The town gossip caught wind of the news that you were coming to Lancaster."

"How did Mrs. Wenter find out?"

Jed threw back his head and laughed. "So you remember her! She hasn't changed, but this once I can't be upset with her."

"I wish that Mama and Papa could have been here. They wanted us to be married, and they often felt as if they were to blame."

"No, Rose, it wasn't their fault. Circumstances kept us apart, and circumstances are what are bringing us back together. We have lost two years of our lives together, but the important thing is we are together. We will live each day as a new day and give Hope the best life as we can."

"Then you're not upset with having Hope with us? Most newly married couples don't start out with a ready-made family."

"Rose, she is a part of you. I will love her as if she was my own, and that's the way it will be. Your parents would be very proud of how you are raising her. I think that they would agree with your decision to come back to Lancaster. I know, for a fact, I do."

"Jed, I knew that you would feel this way! We will have to make some changes to the way the house is set up, but it won't be much."

Jed stopped in his tracks as though a thought just occurred to him. "Rose, what will she call me?"

"She will call you whatever feels right for her. We are not going to make her call us anything. She does call me Mama though."

Jed contemplated for a moment and then said, "It doesn't matter what she calls me just as long as the two of you are a part of my life."

Rose squeezed his arm, and together they walked up the steps of the church to the altar to be married by Parson Jones. Someone offered Rose a beautiful bouquet of daisies.

As they stood in front of the church, Jed's heart was bursting. He had dreamed about this for so long that it hardly seemed real. He looked at Rose from the corner of his eyes and noticed, although it hardly seemed possible, that she was even more beautiful than before. They stood before Parsons Jones, and a very audible Mrs. Wenter blew her nose sniffling loudly into her Sunday-best handkerchief.

Even the parson was in his element, and for the first time, Jed thought he did a remarkable job. Poor parson! He couldn't bore everyone with his dry-as-dust sermon because he wasn't prepared for it. He stuck to the very traditional service of marriage, and the whole ceremony was over in less than six minutes.

After the simple ceremony, Jed and Rose accepted well wishes from those who had gathered in the church. His father grinned as he shook his son's hand, and pointing to the buggy, he said, "I thought that you would probably need a ride for the two of you home."

Accepting his father's handshake he nodded his thanks to his father. Turning to Rose, he scooped her up and carried his bride to the waiting buggy and gently lifted her up. Rose reached down to take Hope, but Jenny beat her to the little girl. "Not for a couple of days." she said, "She's coming home to stay with Grandma and Grandpa. She needs to get to know us!"

So with a wave to all of the well-wishers, Jed picked up the reins, chirruped to the horse, and headed toward their home. With hearts full, the horse, in his own accord, gaily trotted with an air of importance. Even he seemed to know that this occasion was of great circumstance, and he sped proudly toward Jed's home.

They soon reached the little stream that held many beautiful memories. Jed pulled the horse next to a tree and tied it up. He helped his bride down, and together they walked to stream that was nearly dry and sat down on some large rocks.

She smiled as she looked at him and said, "Remember the last time we were here, Jed? A lot of water has gone under the bridge, so to speak. I am so happy that we are together again, and there is nothing that can separate us now."

Jed thought only a moment before responding to Rose. "Yes, that was a long two years. I thought my life would never be the same, and now, of course, it won't be. There will be nothing that we can't handle."

"You were on my mind constantly, Jed. Everything that I did back East seemed to take so long. All I wanted was to get Hope and myself back here to you."

Jed laughed. "I kept on with my work and continued to get things done as if you were coming back here someday. Each time I worked on a fence or a project for the stable or house, I would ask myself how you would have done that."

"It is so perfect here, Jed. The Sunday-afternoon buggy rides always seemed to end up here. I thought of this spot as ours."

"Me too. But as pleasant as this all is, I still have chores to do, and the sun seems to start to go down far too soon each day."

With that, he jumped up and helped Rose to her feet and held her for a long minute before walking to the buggy. After helping her up, he untied the horse and climbed in beside her and trained the horse in the direction of his and Rose's farm.

Chapter 2

As she slept, Jed was looking at his wife's face, scrutinizing how she could be so beautiful. She was just as he remembered her. Her mouth was open ever so slightly, and every once in a while, she would release a little sigh. Waking up, she smiled as she looked at her husband. She hadn't had such a comfortable sleep since she left Lancaster two years ago.

Stretching, she laughed and said, "How long have you been looking at me?"

"Not long enough. I'm afraid the sun beat me up this morning."

"Well, sleepyhead, check the chicken house and bring me in some eggs. I'm going to see if I pass your inspection as a cook." With that, she headed toward the kitchen and started a quick fire in the stove. She watched for a moment as Jed made his way to the chicken coop and thought how lucky she was to finally be here. She made her way back to the bedroom to change from her nightgown into a work dress.

Finding the potatoes, she began to fry them and was setting the table as Jed came into the house with the prized eggs. Grinning, he tossed her one.

Reacting quickly, she caught it and laughed. "That's enough! I may not be as lucky next time. Wash up, breakfast is soon ready."

By the time Jed washed up, the eggs and potatoes were ready, and for the first time, the two set down to their first meal together.

"Well, Mrs. Carlson, what do you have planned for the day?"

"I must say, Mr. Carlson, it is a joy to be called Mrs. Carlson. Today, I believe I'm going to take a look at the garden space and plot out my vegetables. I'll need to make a trip to Lancaster at some point to see it I can pick up seeds."

"I think that I can help you with that. Mother left several different types of seeds a few days ago. I thought that was rather odd that she would do that. She has always given me whatever fresh produce I needed."

"Well, now she's planning on helping me to get started with preserving vegetables. But if we stay here and visit all day, I'll not get a thing done."

With that she picked up the empty plates and busied herself in the kitchen while Jed headed to the horses' stalls. He watered them and carried the oats from the oats bin and curried the animals as they ate. Every once in a while, she would glance out the window to see if she could catch a glimpse of her young man. Each time she saw him, she would smile to herself and know that she had made the right decision. Yes, life was going to be good. She took a gander out of the opposite side of the room and noticed a small white building about a half a mile away. It seemed to be in the middle of nowhere. Wondering, she thought it would be worth a trip to find Jed and ask him about it. She quickly finished her morning chores and headed out in the beautiful, large morning. She stopped about midway from the shed and stood breathing in the fresh air. She closed her eyes and felt the beauty of the day. She was so lost in her thoughts she didn't hear Jed come up behind her and place his arms around her.

"Hey, lovely lady. Are you happy here?"

Still holding her, she turned to face him and smiled a breathtaking smile. "Yes, Jed, I am. Everywhere I look, it is beautiful. Each direction offers a picture that has been etched in my mind for two years. This is exactly what sustained me for the time while I was gone. Each night as I lay in bed with Hope beside me, I hoped and prayed that she would grow up on this farm. Yes, Jed, I am happy."

"Then so am I. And I'll be content to be here as long as you are."

The remembering why she came out, Rose said, "Jed, what is that white building I see about a half mile out of the back window?"

Looking to see where she pointed, he replied, "Oh, that's Wilson School."

"The Wilson School? I don't remember that. Is that new?"

"Yes, it is. It was just new this spring. The Wilson family practically needed one for themselves. They have seven kids, so old man Wilson decided it was time to use the set-aside acre that the Homestead Act set up every two miles. Besides, there are three other families that will send their kids there."

"Hope will go there when she's old enough. I'll be able to watch her walk to school. This place is so perfect for us!"

Jed smiled and nodded at his lovely bride. "Rose, I want to show you the stables. The horse is going to foal soon."

He opened the stable door for Rose. She stepped inside and allowed her eyes to adjust to the darkness before she went any further. Jed opened the door wide and set a bucket in front on the door to prop it open. There in the corner, in her stall, was the mare. Jed spoke gently to her. "It's just about time isn't it, Sugar? We'll be extra careful with you until it is over with."

Rose approached cautiously. She sensed that the horse was not bothered by her, so she touched her nose gently. "How much longer do you think it will be, Jed?"

"Probably today or tomorrow."

"Will you need to be here when she has the colt?"

"I hope to be just in case she has trouble."

"May I be here too?"

"Yes, I think that she can tell you are a kindred spirit, but let me come in here first. She is used to me."

Rose took a quick look around. "Where are the hens?"

"They're in the back of the horse shed. I fixed up a spot for them when the mare was getting close to foaling. They appeared to irritate her with their presence. Want to see them?"

"Of course, I do."

Hand in hand, they walked to the back of the shed. Rose shaded her eyes as she peered into the lean-to. She could see the nests that the hens had made for their eggs. She walked in and thought how much work it must have taken Jed to set up this little area for the chickens. Some of the nests were empty, but a few of them were occupied. As she was getting ready to leave the lean-to, one hen ruffled her feathers and cackled the success of her endeavors. As Rose stepped back over the threshold, she put her hand under the chicken and pulled out a warm brown egg. Holding it in her hand, she turned to Jed and smiled. "I can't wait for Hope to be a part of our farm."

Jed nodded his head in agreement, and together they walked back to the house both thinking their own thoughts and each happy in where they were. The day could not have been more perfect.

Leaving his wife at the door, he asked her what her plans were for the rest of the day.

"Well, I think that with your help we should think about starting a garden. Have you the time to help me work it up?"

At that moment Jed realized that things were going to be a lot different around there. He thought about the multitude of jobs that he needed to get done but he also knew that he would help Rose out with whatever she needed. Nodding, he headed to his work until she was ready for his help. He turned back to the stables and left Rose to her plan her own schedule for the day. She watched Jed walk away from the house and then entering the house started her day by familiarizing herself with the kitchen area.

Often, in the course of the morning, she glimpsed out of the window to the south. She found herself unconsciously looking for Jed and wondering what was he did all day long. Walking into the bedroom, she quickly made that room neat and began to plan the noon meal.

Looking into the pantry, she noticed how everything was definitely lacking a woman's hand. There seemed to be no rhyme or reason regarding the organization of the dishes and other cooking necessities. Bending down, she pulled out a loaf pan for bread and a bowl for mixing up a batch next to the dishes. Biting her lower lip, she contemplated whether she should stop and make a loaf of fresh bread. Deciding to, she began searching for the necessary ingredients. When she found the flour, she made a mental note to organize her kitchen better. But for the meantime, she continued to guess as to where to find the items she needed. The baking for supper should really come first. She could tend to the straightening of the cupboards later as she had time. Salt pork, along with potatoes, for the main course would be good. Perhaps, she would make a pieplant. She had seen a clump of it next to the corner near the back of the house. Rose hadn't noticed that by the edge of the house before. She would ask Jed about that later.

Surprisingly, the morning went by quickly, and Rose found dinner was ready when Jed came in at noon.

As the two of them sat at the table, Rose questioned Jed about the pieplant that she found near the house.

"You know, I wondered why mother transplanted it there early in the spring. She has a big bed of it, and when she offered to put some near the house, I thought that was pretty odd. She usually just sent me home a piece or two on Sunday nights."

Rose laughed. "Yes, I think that your mother was smarter than either one of us. She helped us get our home ready without either one of us knowing it."

Jed agreed, "Yes, she has always had a way of knowing what I needed even before I did."

"Oh, that reminds me." Rose got up from the table and located the small gallon-sized butter churn. "We don't have a cow, so what did you use this for?"

"Where did you find it? I have never seen it."

"Down on the bottom of the cupboard. You didn't know you had it?"

"Nope, probably my mother brought it."

As they were contemplating this, they heard a horse and a rider come up the lane. Going to the window they saw Jed's younger brother sauntering up the lane, leading a cow. He hopped down from his horse as he approached the stable. As Jed and Rose met him, he handed the cow's rope to Jed.

"Here's a wedding present from the folks. Ma said there was a churn in the cupboards for you to make your own butter." As he said that, Jed and Rose looked at one another and smiled silently acknowledged what was stated earlier.

"But the folks didn't have a cow like that. Where did they get it?"

Mr. Wilson traded it to Pa. Pa helped him get his crops in last fall in exchange for it. I went to get it this morning."

"Would you like to come in for pie? I just made it this morning."

"Can't. Pa said to get home, but I can take a piece to eat on the way." So ducking inside, Rose brought out a slice to Jake, and thanking her, he pulled on the halter and started his horse toward home. Stopping for a moment, he turned in the saddle and hollered over his shoulder, "Forgot to tell you Ma will bring Hope back day after tomorrow."

What those parting words, Rose and Jed went to their respective tasks. As Rose entered the house, she looked about for something to place Hope in for her bedtime. Not finding anything suitable, she walked out to where Jed was working and asked him for suggestions. He was leaning against the horse's stable and chewing on a piece of straw.

"How about the packing box that the new saddle came in? It should be just about right for her."

"That would be perfect! I'll fold a couple of quilts on the bottom of it, and then I can tuck her blankets under the quilts so she will stay covered at night."

She went back toward the house and wandered about the trees before she thought that she had better get back to work.

Chapter 3

Jenny brought Hope home to Jed and Rose's farm. Already the little girl had become very attached to her new grandma. As they got closer to the house, she could see Rose and very delightedly clapped her hands and giggled out loud. Rose was as happy to see her sister. She lifted her from the horse and twirled her around until she was breathless from exertion. Jed watched from a distance and smiled broadly at the reunion of the two sisters.

Strolling over to his mother, he helped her down and greeted her warmly. Rose was anxious to show her new mother-in-law the changes she had made to the house in the past two days. Jed watched as the two women and Hope walked to the house, laughing as they went. His heart flooded with warmth at the happiness that was shared by his mother and Rose. Rose missed her mother. Even though her mother was gone, Jenny would begin to fill up a void that had been in Rose's heart.

They first went into the bedroom, and Rose pulled out the trundle bed that she had prepared for Hope. Hope climbed over the edge of the box and covered herself up so Rose could see how well she fit. Jenny and Rose left her to explore her new space and checked out the kitchen. She showed Jed's mother how well everything was rearranged and how much handier it all was.

"Jed was busy every moment that you were gone. He never lost sight of the possibility that you would be coming back."

"Nor did I, Jenny. At first it seemed impossible, but I realized that I couldn't raise Hope on my own. I did meet a young banker who would have made a home for Hope and me very comfortable. I could have had the finest silks and a servant to take care of the household. I could have been happy, but not like Jed and I are going to be. I wanted to live a life that is full of promise and love and, yes, adventure. Back East, nothing would have been expected of me. I would only have to take care of Hope."

Jenny looked at her daughter-in-law closely. "I think that you are going to be happy with your decision, don't you?"

"Yes, already I am. I have loved Jed for so long and hard. I would have never gotten over him. What kind of life would that have been had I married the banker? It wouldn't have been fair to Hope, him, or myself knowing that I love Jed. It would have been tolerable, but I wanted more for Hope and myself."

"Yes, I think that things will work out with the three of you. Ben and I are close by if you ever need a thing."

"Jenny, you have helped us so much already. You helped to get my home ready and to get us here, and Jed didn't even have a clue."

Jenny laughed. "If you had seen Jed while you were gone, you might have changed your mind about coming. He was not a delight to be around. Ben and I helped as much as we were able, but we had to just let the storm pass so to speak."

"Do you think I should tell Jed about the young banker?"

"I don't think you should keep secrets from each other, but I will also add this. I would wait until he asked you. He is a pretty confident young man who knows what he wants in life. He is also very sensible. He knows that you have chosen to be with him, and in the long run, that is what is important."

Rose replied, "I think that makes sense. I don't want to leave him out of anything, but I think I will wait until he asks."

"I think that we should check on Hope. She may have gotten into something. She is pretty quiet. Don't you think, Rose?"

"Right you are!"

With that they peeked in the bedroom door and saw that the little girl with dust on her face and long curls over her eyes had fallen fast asleep. Rose covered her with a light shawl and closed the door behind them as they left.

"Well, that answers one question. I know at least she will be comfortable in her bed."

Jenny smiled and said, "I had better get going. Ben and I really enjoyed having her. Sophie was delighted to have someone younger around to boss around and to mother. I hope you will let us keep her again. It is good for the two of you as well."

Rose thanked her and, peering out of the kitchen window at Jed, saw that Jenny's horse was tied behind the buggy that they had come home in as newlyweds.

"I see that Jed has the rig ready."

"Yes, don't forget Sunday dinner at the home place after church."

"Jenny, you are so good to us. I am so happy that Hope and I have you and your family in our lives. I am so grateful that Hope will have grandparents who love her." Rose wiped the tears from her eyes.

Jenny hugged her, and together they walked out to the buggy. Jenny climbed aboard, waving to Jed and Rose, spoke to the horses and was soon down the lane.

Jed stood next to Rose with his arm around her waist, feeling very grateful that he had two such women in his life.

Rose felt that gratitude and returned his hug. "I don't deserve to be so happy. Your parents are so good to Hope and me."

"That's a two-way street, love. They are very happy with you also."

"I hope that I never disappoint them or you, either, Jed."

"Be yourself, Rose. That is all any of us ever ask."

"You know, Jed, we have been here not even a week, but it feels like home."

"That is because, my dear, it is. Now get to making my supper while I finish up chores." With that, he turned back to the horse shed to make the animals comfortable for the night and to check on the progress of the horse that would soon foal.

Rose smiled, watching him walk away. She turned and headed back to the house to prepare the evening meal. She had barely started when she heard Jed walking up to the house.

Jed said, "I'm going to sit in the stable with the mare. Do you want to come out? Thought that you would like to be there."

Rose took off her apron, checked on the sleeping Hope, and dashed out to the horse shed.

Jed was already there stroking the weary horse. Hearing Rose near the doorway, he quietly told her to sit on the bale of hay directly inside the door. Rose took her spot and listened to Jed comforting the mare. The mare had raised her head slightly when Rose entered but found no threat to the woman as she came in.

Rose was very grateful for that. She wanted to be there with Jed and the mare to witness the wonderful miracle of birth. She had not noticed how big the mare was. Lying down seemed to emphasize the roundness of her baby pouch.

Jed spoke softly, "She seems to be breathing a little harder that she did with her first colt. I hope that it is not too much for her."

Rose whispered, "She will be all right, won't she? Is there anything I can get you?"

Jed shook his head. "I think that it will be awhile yet. Perhaps you should finish supper. I'll eat and then come back out here to be with her. She seems to like me here."

Rose nodded and quietly exited the stable. Upon entering the house, she heard Hope was awake and went to pick up the little girl from her nap. Hope grinned at Rose and happily outstretched her arms to be picked up. Rose kissed her and carried her out of the bedroom and placed her in chair. "Hmm, it seems as if I need to find a more suitable chair."

Glancing around, she spotted two heavy books and placed them on the Hope's chair. Tying a dishtowel around the little girl and the back of the chair, she pushed it up to the table. Rose offered her sister tidbits of the noon meal and continued to get supper for Jed and herself.

Supper was ready quickly as Rose knew that Jed wanted to get back to the business at hand. Jed came in when she called. Washing up outside in the basin that was waiting on a chair, he dried with the towel and came in.

Rose looked at Jed and thought how handsome he looked even though his hair was a mess and that his clothes smelled like the stable.

He noticed her staring at him and smiled, "Did you think that it would be like this?"

She laughed. "Was I that obvious?" she shared her thoughts with him.

He, too, then laughed and grabbed her by the waist and swung her around.

"Jed, not in front of Hope!" They both looked at Hope laughing and clapping her hands, watching in delight at the two of them.

"Well, that answers your question. She likes it, and so do I!"

Rose replied, "You two! I am going to be surrounded by hopeless romantics. I think I like it too!"

Rose showed Jed the trundle bed and said how well Hope had slept that afternoon. "She was probably exhausted with all the attention she got it the folks. Plus, she had Sophie to keep up with, and that was perhaps the most fun of all," Rose said.

Jed sat down as Rose served the meal. Jed was ready to reach for the meat platter when Rose looked at him. He had no idea what she meant by that look.

"Jed, we want to make sure Hope grows up the right way. If we wish for her to grow up in a loving home I think we need to show her we are thankful for what we have."

Jed pulled his hand back. "You know I was brought up with a table grace, but I have been alone so much I got out of practice," he explained.

"Yes, it is easy to do that. The longer you go without the prayer, the easier it is to go without it. We can take turns."

Jed looked nervous, and Rose caught that expression. "It's okay. I will lead it for a while, then when you are comfortable with it you can lead."

Jed thought to himself, *That may be awhile.*

Rose led the table grace and then encouraged Jed to help himself, which he did.

The newlyweds chatted easily throughout the meal, pausing several times to keep Hope satisfied with what was before her.

"How does the mare look, Jed?"

"I think that she is ready to give birth. If she hasn't by tomorrow, then I'll go after my father and have him take a look at her. He has been through this much more than I have."

"Will you stay out with her during that night?" asked Rose.

"Probably. I wasn't there when she birthed her first one, but she seems to be having a more difficult time with this one. I want to watch her especially close."

"I'll see if I can find one of your old blankets that you can use tonight in the stable. That should at least help a bit."

He smiled at her. "If you wake up in the night, come out and check on us to see how we are progressing."

"I sure will, Mr. Carlson."

"If you can find some clean rags that I could use, I would appreciate it."

"I think I know where to look. As soon as you are finished, go ahead and see how the mare is doing, and we will bring them out shortly."

"Thanks, but if Hope comes, you might need to wait outside the stable door. I don't want Sugar to be frightened."

"Oh, I never thought of that. She might be a little excited at the prospect of seeing the horse so close up. We'll be careful."

Throughout the meal, Hope kept her eyes on Jed, wondering about him and how he was going to fit into her and Rose's lives. Jed, on the other hand, kept looking sideways and wondered how she would fit into his life. She was better at staring him down than he was her.

Finally, Jed turned toward her. "Well, pumpkin, it looks as is we both have some adjustments to make."

She laughed when he called her a pumpkin. That one word sealed a relationship that would last a lifetime. She liked Jed and learned to love him not only as a father but as a lifelong friend.

Chapter 4

After the supper meal, Jed grabbed his hat and headed outside. Rose was anxious to be out there as well so she hurried through dishes and searched for the needed rags for Jed. She picked up Hope from her makeshift high chair and, holding her by the hand, walked out to the stable. Hope had plenty of energy as a result of her big afternoon nap and happily skipped beside Rose.

Shortly before they got to the stable, Rose stopped and knelt down in front of Hope. She looked at her and explained what they were about to do.

"Now, Hope, there is a mama horse getting ready to have her baby. We have to be very quiet so that she will continue to rest until the baby is born. Do you understand what I mean?"

Hope jumped up and down and clapped at the thought of seeing the baby horse. "Oh yes!" she shouted. "I want to see the baby!"

Okay, thought Rose, *maybe this isn't such a good idea. We had better just walk to the door and hand these to Jed*. She took Hope's hand and finished their walk to the stable.

Jed met them at the door. "I heard you tried, but I had better take the cloths. You two can peek inside. Sugar is facing the other way. As long as she doesn't hear you, you can stand in the doorway."

Taking the rags, he stepped back inside, calmly talking to the horse. He took his place by its head and continued to talk soothingly to her.

Hope was in awe of the horse that was lying on its side. She somehow knew it was the right time to be quiet. She pointed to the big round belly of the mare and whispered to Rose, "Mama, did she eat a lot? Is that why she doesn't feel good?"

Rose smiled back at the little girl and said. "No, she is going to have a baby. When she has the baby she will be smaller and feel better."

Hope nodded her understanding and continued to watch for something unsure of what it was but still watching. After a short time, she and Rose moved to the bale of hay and, as still as little mice, continued to watch the mare and its owner.

Jed stepped away from the horse and spoke quietly to his wife, "I think that she will deliver, if she is able to, within the few hours."

Rose nodded and whispered back, "I think that I'll wash up Hope and get her ready for bed. She has had a busy last couple of days." She put Hope down and let her run to the house.

As she washed Hope's face, she looked at Rose with such love and trust that Rose felt tears spring to her eyes. She thought how sad it was for Hope not to know their parents. They were wonderful people. She vowed to herself again that she would take the very best care that she could of her. After slipping on her sister a little nightgown, Rose sat on the edge of the big bed and gently moved her body back and forth while softly singing to her. The rocking motion, along with the soft lullaby that Rose sang, put Hope to sleep in a few minutes. As the little girl lay in her arms, Rose looked at the exhaustion on her face and then gently laid her in her trundle bed. Casting one last look at the sleeping child, Rose shut the bedroom door behind herself. She quickly cleaned up the supper mess, and then stealing one last look at Hope, she left the house and went to the stable.

Jed acknowledged her as she came in and whispered, "Just about there."

Rose nodded her head and sat upon the bale. She sat for nearly three hours, checking often on Hope, who was still sleeping. When she came back from checking on Hope for the third time, she heard commotion in the stable. She quickened her steps, then she entered and took up her position on the hay.

Jed continued speaking to the horse in low tones. "It's all right Sugar, almost there."

With one big exertion from the horse, Jed could see the head of the foal as it attempted to enter the world. The horse lifted its head. The side of the horse heaved, and the baby was born. Jed took the clean rags and wiped off the baby's mouth and nose so it could begin to breath. Rose smiled and clapped her hands, making no sound.

He pushed the foal up to the mare, and the mare continued the cleanup process. But still the mare didn't stand.

"Come on, girl, you need to get up to clean your baby."

The mare continued to lay down.

"If I didn't know better, I would guess that she hasn't had the baby yet. Look at her stomach."

Rose looked, and while they were both wondering, the mare exerted herself and, with another big effort, delivered a second colt. Both Rose and Jed looked in amazement. Cleaning that one up as well, the mare now stood after resting only a few moments. Her work had just begun. Rose left the stable and waited for Jed.

He came out soon and spoke to Rose. "I have never seen that before. I thought she looked awfully big but never thought it would be two of them!"

"Can she take care of two?"

"Sure. She has already had 1 one colt. She knows what to do." Checking to make sure she had water, he closed the door walked to the house with Rose.

"I'll look in on her later and give her feed then."

Washing up, Jed and Rose quietly went to the bedroom and fell asleep.

Jed woke up halfway through the night, and immediately his mind went to the welfare of the horse. He dressed hurriedly and grabbed his jacket before heading to the barn. Cautiously, he opened the stable door and peered in. His lantern helped him to adjust to the dark. He could see the eyes of the mare and heard the sleeping sounds of the colts. He put out some oats and brushed his horse in appreciation for her hard work.

"You did pretty good, old girl. Had to deliver two babies. You were always a bit better than any other horse I knew. You rest up now. I'll check you in a few hours." With that, he left the shed and joined Rose and Hope as they both slumbered, Hope with light breathing and Rose with heavier sounds. Not a snore really, but definitely louder. He thought it would be better if he didn't mention that to her.

Turning over, he closed his eyes for a few hours of uninterrupted sleep. When he awoke, it was with his face to a full sun. Both Rose and Hope were no where to be seen. He did smell, however, coffee and heard the sound of salt pork frying. Hurriedly he dressed and checked his timepiece. Seven o'clock. Holy smokes! He couldn't remember ever sleeping this long!

Opening the bedroom door, he was greeted by a little girl who ran into his arms, saying, "The pumpkin beat you up this morning!"

"Yes, you did!" And with that he tickled her until the noise was so loud Rose begged them to stop.

"Breakfast is ready, Jed. Would you be so kind as to put your little pumpkin on her throne?"

Hearing that, Hope laughed again and allowed Jed to tie her to the chair.

After they all sat down, Rose began to lay out her day. "I need to plant some seeds. The ground is so dry. Have we had much rain here?"

"No," replied Jed. "We had very little snow this winter, maybe six inches or less. I need to sow the oats, but I'm afraid the seeds won't grow. The weather has been nice, but no rain to speak of."

"You've got to plant. We need crops to sell, and we have animals to feed. Won't the spring rains start soon?"

"Yes, you're right. I'm just feeling lazy after the last few nights. I'll work on that project today."

"I wonder if I should put the pumpkins seed out first."

"No," said Jed, "wait until I get the corn in, then we'll plant pumpkins when the corn gets about knee high. They'll grow well in the cornfield."

"But I want to see them as they grow. Couldn't I put a couple of them by the house?"

Jed laughed at her. "Not unless you want them to take over any flowers that you have growing. Pumpkins really branch out."

"Oh, okay, maybe I'll just put out some of the early vegetables. Hope, you want to help Mama?"

Hope kicked at the table's underside enthusiastically.

Rose laughed. "I take that as a yes."

Jed hurriedly left the table, and Rose got up to finish the dishes and get her day organized.

"Come on, Hope let's go check out the soil that Daddy worked up."

Jed was just outside the kitchen door and smiled. That sounded so good. "I hope I make a good daddy." He said it out loud, but it was for his own benefit and not for anyone else to hear.

He was just getting to the stable to check his horse when he heard Rose scream.

Racing toward the sound, his mind raced as well. What was wrong? He found the two girls in the area in the back of the house. There he found Rose on a stump while Hope was hanging on to a garter snake and shaking it.

It was probably not smart for Jed to laugh, but he couldn't help it. "It's just a little snake, Rose. They are good to have in the garden."

Rose was not prepared to be convinced. "Jed, you get that snake out of here! It might bite Hope!"

"I'll take it away, but they are good for getting rid of pests. Here, Hope, give Daddy the snake." He hadn't planned on saying that, but that word came out so easily. He looked up at Rose to see if she had noticed. She had, and she smiled at the thought. She came down from the stump after Jed threw away the snake.

He knelt next to Hope and said, "Pumpkin, sometimes snakes can be bad. So until you know which ones are, you are not to pick any up. Do you understand?"

With round eyes, she nodded and looked directly into his she asked, "Could he eat me up?"

"No." Jed laughed. "But there are snakes that bite. Okay?"

Again, she nodded and bent down to dig some more in the dirt.

"Jed, you handled that wonderfully. But let's be clear. I don't want her to pick up any snake."

Jed nodded, but he hurried out to the field so he could laugh in private. He then knelt and ran the soil through his calloused hand. It was dry, but it always rained when he needed it. With the warm weather soon to be coming, he needed the moisture for his crops to grow. Certainly, it was too early to worry about the harvest. He had spent the last two weeks working up the soil. It appeared ready. He would just go by faith. The rains would come—they always did. They would again this year.

Heading back to the stable he got his sower bag, placed the seeds in it, and began to plant. He started at the north end of the field, walking and sweeping his hands full of oats seeds, making sure it was a steady motion. He had raised oats two years ago, and his field was one of the finest stands of oat fields in the area. Even his father had commented on how well he had done. He realized that he was twenty-four years old when his father said that. And that comment still made him feel good. He respected the older man very much and thought how fortunate he was to grow up in the family that he did. He renewed his determination to raise the same type of family that he grew up in.

Every so often, he would glance back at the house to see if he could spot Rose or Hope. They must be busy in the garden or the house. As he approached the homestead, he could see that there were clothes hanging on the line, frilly ones. He felt nervous. What if someone rode up to the house and saw those hanging outside for anyone to see? He realized that wasn't a realistic thought. Oh course, where else should she hang them? Hmm. This was going to be way different with females around. But the more he thought about that, the more he knew that he wouldn't change it for any amount of money.

He wasn't finished with the oat field until it was nearly dark. He finally saw Rose holding on to Hope's hand and walking toward the edge of the building site.

"I was beginning to wonder if all was well. We've missed you today. I have supper waiting. Do you think you'll be able to come in soon? Hope has already eaten, and she wanted to say good night to you before I put her to bed."

"Sure. I'll feed the horses first. Won't take me but ten minutes. Then I'll wash up and come in."

"Great, I'll put her nightdress on, and we'll be waiting for you."

With that, the two turned and walked up to the house. Jed watched them go and thought to himself how much Hope looked like Rose, and he supposed that Hope was what Rose looked like when she was that age. He hurried through the feeding of the horses and thought he may as well lock the chickens up for the night at the same time.

The twin colts were frisking about in the stable. Tomorrow, he would let them out in the small pasture to see how they were going to act in the open spaces. As he watered the horses, he leaned against the stall and thought how his life had changed so quickly in such a short time. Life had been pretty simple when he was a bachelor. Now he had a ready-made family, and life was about to get very complicated.

With those thoughts, he took one last glance around the stable, making sure all was well for the night, and went outside, shutting the door behind him. He blew out the lantern and walked toward his happy home, a pretty wife and child, and a good meal. He didn't think that life could get any better than this.

Chapter 5

For the first few weeks of spring, no one thought much about the lack of rain. Rain had always come in time for the planting of the seeds. A small amount of moisture helped the oats make a stand. By the time June had arrived, no significant amount of rain had fallen. The Fourth of July, the crops were barely three inches high. It seemed as if the tiny plants were afraid to grow. Jed often walked down the rows of the miniature crops wondering, worrying, and saying little. Rose could see how much the conversation about the crops bothered him, so she quit asking about them.

Jed knew how important it was to produce a crop each year. It would soon be time to make payment on the mortgage, and there was no money in which to pay it. He sought advice from his father.

"I don't know, Jed," his father said. "There doesn't seem to be any relief in sight. I have no mortgage, but I need money and my crops to make it through the year until I can plant again."

"How do we make it through the rest of the year? I don't have any money in the bank. I used it to maintain and improve the homestead. What do I tell Rose?"

"Tell her the truth. If she is the woman that I think she is, you'll find she can be very resourceful and able to help your situation out."

"She's worried about her garden. The well is nearly dry, and her flowers are all wilted up. I feel like a failure."

"There are a lot of men in your situation. This dry weather is has been taking its toll on many families."

"Have you heard of any jobs in town or men hiring?"

"No, not really. The railroad that was going to be built near the town is going farther north. So any commerce and transporting of goods will have to be hauled in. A few families have gone back East. I imagine that we can make out for the year but it will be tight. We might as well work on things that the dry weather won't affect. There is nothing to do in the fields, so we might as well get our wood cut for the winter. Maybe we can sell some."

"I have no extra hay to speak of. I was planning on pasturing them. But with the weather so dry, I can't depend on that anymore. I'll have to keep moving them, but even then the fresh grass will run out. I can't make it through until next harvest though."

"You know, Jed, this dry spell is only a regional thing. They say a hundred miles south and a hundred miles north, there is all the water they need."

"It will be hard on everybody if we don't get some rain. The storekeepers and the other businesses depend on the area farmers to buy from them. They can't afford to stay open if they can't sell anything."

"Are they able to carry anybody?"

"Not likely. Each man has been asked to pay up their outstanding debt. Some do that when they get their crop in each fall. If there are no crops, then there is no way for the farmers to pay off their obligations."

"I imagine that some farmers will sell off their livestock in hopes to stay solvent."

"Rose loves the animals. The chickens can pretty much fend for themselves with the grasshoppers and what little water they need from the creek. They don't lay as many eggs and Rose depends upon that for daily meals."

"There was a man who came through on the stagecoach yesterday. He was heading for the East. Appeared to have some money as he was dressed well. He was looking for a buggy so he could take a swing through northern Iowa looking for a place to set up a business. Said the crops near Osage were as good as they had ever been according to his brother who lives there."

"Are you thinking of selling yours?"

"Yes, I am. I hate to part with it, but I need to put food on the table too. In a way, farmers are a little better off than most people. They still have a limited source of vegetables that they can raise. Farmers have always pretty much depended upon themselves right from the start."

"But you waited your whole life to have a buggy. You and mother have worked hard for that. She would hate to give it up."

"Yes, but we have talked about it, and we were made an offer of thirty-five dollars for it. Not exactly a top-of-the-line offer, but it will put food on out table for a couple of months. I've decided to sell it."

Jed couldn't believe his ears. Things were changing so fast. One day, this future on the farm with Rose seemed so bright; the next day, a huge cloud hung over it.

"Even though," his father continued, "we might get a crop next year, we still have the problem of limited business with the railroad being rerouted. Did you know that the stage will terminate its services from here? They'll be going north with the railroad. Lancaster will no longer be the county seat. That will be in Sigourney."

Jed shook his head in disbelief. He had an inkling that things would be different because of the lack of the winter precipitation. He wasn't prepared for anything like this.

"I think what we should do," said the elder Carlson, "is to let the horses graze down by the creek every day. They can at least find the water that they need. There is a small spring that should satisfy that need. The grass is still green all along the banks because of the water source. But I don't expect that to be a viable source for grazing very long. We need to be able to keep our horses especially if we are to continue to farm once the drought is over. The cow should be able to make out down there as well. It will probably quit giving milk."

"It has already," said Jed. "Hope cries for it especially at night."

"I imagine so. But look around your homestead, Jed. If there is anything of value and you can do without it, see if you can sell it. It may be enough to help you through a week or two for food. We can eek by, but it will be a sacrifice for all of us. It all depends on how frugally we want to live."

"It's a pretty bleak picture, isn't it? I hate to worry Rose with all the details."

"Rose probably already knows. I am sure she is thinking all the time with her pretty little head of how she can help with your dilemma. Let her into your thoughts, Jed. If will be better for the both of you."

"Yeah, you're right. I'll talk to her tonight."

"And you know, Jed, Lancaster is not the only place to make a living and raise your family."

"But you've always lived here. Your father was one of the original founders of the town."

"That's true. But there are other places to live where there is no drought and that are just as nice, if not better.

This town was my father's dream. I thought it was mine too. But it is only a place, a location where we first hung up our hats. If we can't make it here, then I'm willing to look for a place where I can. You may want to think about that too."

"You've already thought about that haven't you, Father?"

"Yes, I have. You're mother is very happy here. She loves her home, but she also knows that sometimes there are situations that are out of our control. And the weather is one of them."

"But look how long it has taken me to build up my farm. I have spent four years toiling over the rocks and tree stumps, battling the storms and the grasshoppers."

"I see where you are coming from, Jed. But you know the Swenson brothers have been here for at least thirty years. Everything they have is invested in their land. Think of all the improvements they have made on their property. They own their land free and clear. Last year, hail wiped them out, and this year, it is the drought. We, at least, had a fairly decent crop last year. They didn't."

"Have you heard about them looking to leave?"

"Well, they are both in their late fifties. It will be kind of hard to start over. But I'm thinking they will try."

"I had better head back to the farm. Rose will be worried. I don't think that we will be at church until it rains. I'm thinking that the horses need to conserve their energy. We probably won't walk in this heat, either. It is too far for

Hope, and she is getting too heavy to carry for any amount of time."

"That's another thing I forgot to mention. Parson Jones packed up and went back East. People couldn't afford to put any money in the collection plate, and he needed to put food on his table as well. It seems as if no one can escape this blasted drought."

On that less-than-cheerful note, Jed bid his father goodbye and headed his horse toward home. He had a lot to think about. He could do without many things, but he wouldn't ask Rose to do the same. What did he have that he could do without in order to help tide him through the next year?

He needed his horses. The two workhorses were needed for the fields if he were ever fortunate to get back into them. He had the twin colts that Hope loved. The cow was sole source for the milk and butter supply, but she was not producing. The chickens were pretty much self-sufficient. They dug around in the dirt in the day. They drank the water that Jed carried from the small pool of water still in the creek. Each of these animals, he was able to care for, and they were helping him to make a living. Should he sell one or all of them? Would Rose understand all of this or would she blame him?

As he looked around the countryside, he knew that the animals were all gone in search of water and food. Even the birds had flown to more attractive places. There was no game left. If they were to survive, there would have to be much sacrifice. Rose knew how to sew, but there would be no money for material. Their clothes could be mended, but even those would wear out. Food was still the main issue, and Jed couldn't think on how to provide for his little family with no money. How did things get to be so bad?

He stopped at the creek where he and Rose would often sit and dream their big dreams and plan their future. It all seemed so bright then. But no one planned on a drought. Lack of water was turning the community upside down. There wasn't a thing that anyone could do about it. Even the creek was only a trickle of water. He remembered how they used to skip the stones across the water. He taught Rose how to do that. She practiced and practiced until she could skip a stone better than he could. He noticed the sun was on its journey into the horizon. Slowly he got up and let the horse lead them both home.

As he got closer to home, everything looked different. He used to look with pride at his accomplishments of each day. He could see the fences that surrounded the pasture and his other two horses trying to find a fresh spot of grass. The colts were lying in the shade of the huge oak tree trying to conserve their energy. Each day when Jed led them to what little water was in the creek, they wrinkled up their lips at the scummy slime that covered the shallow pool. Animals had to endure hardships as well. Each day, Rose placed a bucket under the well pump. During the day, it would drip slowly, so by the end of the day there would be water nearly to the top of the container. At night, she put a new bucket there in order to catch another supply of water. That was all that was collected each day. Two buckets weren't enough. Rose used these buckets in the house for whatever cooking and cleaning she did. It had to be used sparingly. Hope asked for cool drinks of water. Rose nearly cried when she tried to pump up any coolness from the depths of the well. There just wasn't any water there.

Jed took the horses to the brackish water and waited patiently while they drank. Walking them back to the shed, he locked them in for the night. There were horse thieves in the area. People who were ordinarily good people were turning to thievery in any effort to have money to survive. The people who bought the farm animals knew that they were stolen but didn't care as they were bought for ridiculously small amounts of money. They, in turn, sold the horses for much larger amounts in the city. So whether one was a buyer or a seller, both were considered thieves. Locking up the chickens as well, Jed walked up to the house and met Rose on the porch.

Looking at him, Rose knew that the news was not good news. "Your father is worried too, isn't he, Jed?"

He could hardly look at Rose, but he nodded and said, "He thought that we could make a living to the far north or to the south where there have been rains."

She looked around at their perfect little farm. "I do love it so here. I really don't know and understand the finances and the trials of farming, but I do know this. Wherever you think we could make this happen again, I am willing to try. I know that there are those who are heading back East. The blacksmith shop and the saloon are closed down. The store has folded, and the church is just an empty building. Lancaster will be a ghost town in a few years. Small places such as Lancaster don't often bounce back up after such a hardship."

""Yes, you are right. I could probably go north and work for a few months. You would have to stay here to watch the farm and animals. But it would at least be an option."

Rose stamped her foot. Her eyes were wide and angry. "No, Jed! I won't have that. We are either staying here or leaving together. Hope needs her daddy here, and I need my husband with me. Especially now!"

"I know, Rose. It would only be temporary until I can earn enough to last until the next crop. What do you mean especially now?"

Rose smiled. "I was going to tell you at suppertime, but Hope is going to be a big sister."

At first it didn't sink in. But when he noticed her grinning, he realized what she had said. He grabbed her and twirled her around. "You're right!" he said. "We've got to be together! When?"

"In about seven months."

"Will it be a boy?"

She looked at him and laughed. "Yes—or a girl. Let's go in and have our supper."

Chapter 6

Now it seemed as if everything in the world was right again. Not that the farming situation had changed, but with a new baby coming, Jed was willing to sacrifice what he had worked so hard for. It was sad to see the changes to Lancaster, but there was a due season for change, and this seemed to be a time for that to happen. Early one morning, Ben and his family came to see Jed and Rose. They were excited about the news of the baby.

Jed looked at his mother with a curious glance. He said, "You knew, didn't you?"

"Jed, don't worry. Rose didn't tell me. I guessed it. There is something about the way a woman changes when she in with child, and I spotted it in Rose. She probably didn't even know then."

"How could you tell?"

"Well, Jed, I have had five children and have many women friends. I can tell by the glow on her face and the changes to her body. You probably didn't notice them because you are around her all the time. I hadn't seen Rose for over a month since I last saw her, and I could see the change."

Ben added, "Your mother knows these things and much more. Don't ever try to fool her."

"Agreed." Jed nodded. "But why don't you all come in?"

The children wanted to explore the farm with Hope. The adults went into the house to visit.

Ben started. "Jed, an opportunity has come up I think that we should seriously consider."

"What is it?" Jed queried.

"Do you remember Rose's aunt and uncle who used to own the store here?"

"Yes, I remember. What of it?"

He looked at Rose as he said this. "They didn't make it to South Dakota. Thomas took sick up in northern Iowa, and they had to stop until he got better. The people were so kind and helpful to both he and Laura they decided that they had traveled enough. The town where Thomas recuperated was also growing. It is a county seat town as well, but with much more going for it than Lancaster. They opened a general store and were welcomed into the town with open arms. They now have a successful business in only the two years they have been there."

"How does that affect us?"

"Well, Thomas got a homestead that he was working to improve as well as the store. His store is doing so well that they want to give up the claim and work only in the store. He is willing to turn over the claim to his niece, Rose, and you if you would work on the claim for the last three years. You would have to continue to improve the claim in order to prove it should be turned over to you. It would be really the ideal situation to begin all over again. Most people don't have a chance such as this."

"Oh boy, we would have to leave here. What about you and Mother and the kids? What would you do?"

"That's the best part. There is another tract of land adjoining your claim that is for homesteading. He would sign me up for the claim if we are interested."

Jed looked at Rose who was so excited she could hardly contain herself. "Oh, how wonderful it would be to see Aunt Laura and Uncle Thomas again! I have missed them so!"

Jed thought to himself how big a change this would be for them all. Wasn't this a bit hasty? Even if there were crops next year—and there was no guarantee—Lancaster would not have the commerce to help the area farmers. The county seat was gone, no railroad, no stage or incoming mail twice a week. Businesses were few and far between. What would hold him here? There was certainly a lot of blood, sweat, and tears on this farm.

"Could Rose handle the trip in her condition?"

Jenny answered, "The best time would be early on in her pregnancy. Rough roads are hard to take when you are close to your due date."

Rose placed her hands on her stomach and remembered the child her mother had lost on the trail while coming to Lancaster.

"When do we need to decide?"

His father replied, "It would be best to have a roof over our heads before winter. Osage is about 190 miles from here. By the time we sold the farm and packed up our necessities and made the journey, it would be about two months. Thomas said there is a small house on his claim that would be suitable for Jenny, the kids, and me for a month or so. Your little family will stay with Thomas and Laura in the back of their store. They haven't been living there, but they are working on a living space there for the two of them and the three of you until we can get that second house up. During that time, we could put up another shanty that would get us through the winter until we can make a better place the next spring."

"How far from the town are the claims?" Jed asked.

"Yours is a mile and a quarter south of town. Our claim is the back side of that, so that would be almost two miles from Osage. On a good day, you can walk out to the claim to work or ride your horse."

"You and I would be busy with the building of the shanty but we would have to have wood to heat both places over the winter."

"Thomas says there are lots of trees for firewood. We would start Jake and Freddy on that detail until we can help them. With all four of us working, we should be able to make enough wood to last the winter. He says the winters are pretty cold. We should be able to put up a shanty suitable for living in a week or less."

"What about schools? Is there one close for Hope to go in a couple of years?" Rose asked.

"Yes, Sophie will go there. It is only a half of a mile away. The best part of it is that they need a teacher for the school. He wanted to know if Mary was interested. What do you think, Mary? They will pay you a dollar a day. We could use that money to put food on the table until we can grow our own next spring."

Mary's eyes got round. "Do you think I can teach school? I've never done that before."

Jenny answered her daughter with confidence. "Mary, whatever has come your way, you have met it head-on and have done well. We are all embarking into territory that we have never tried. It is a way for us to stay together."

Jenny continued, "I am sure you would find the people around there very happy to get a teacher such as yourself. By the way, Freddy and Jake will be busy with the making of firewood so they won't go to school in the fall."

The two boys heard that last bit of information and whooped and hollered at the thought of no school. Their joy was soon contained as Jenny continued, "They can study at night, and Mary will go over their lessons with them."

Ben added, "It will mean a bit of a sacrifice for us all. At the claim, we will all be living in two rooms. We will be working hard to make things as we want them to be. We may have to do without new dresses or a new plow. But we can get along. Our tempers may be short and the days may be long, but with a lot of work and perseverance, we will accomplish many things in a short time. We can do it."

Each person there was quiet for a time as he or she pondered the changes that would soon take place. The younger children were excited at the prospect of moving. Rose was happy that she could see her aunt and uncle again. Jenny wanted to go wherever Benjamin went. Jed looked at each person in the room and finally cast his eyes upon Rose. She tried to let him decide, but her eyes betrayed her.

Jed sighed and said, "When will we need to be ready?"

A joyous cheer went up from the group as there were many plans to be made.

"I talked to the Swenson brothers, and they have decided not to move. They have a little money saved, and they are going to stick it out. They will farm your land next year if the weather is cooperative. If they do all right, they will send you two hundred dollars for turning the mortgage over to them. As for our land," he said, looking at Jenny, "the banker will buy at for three hundred. He says he is sticking his neck out by doing that. He will send us fifty dollars a year until it is paid off. He can't pay the first payment until next spring."

"Do you trust him, Ben?" asked Jenny.

He looked strangely at her and said, "Jenny, I am surprised at you! He's a banker. Of course, I don't!'

The family laughed, even Hope, who was only laughing because everybody else did.

Jenny said, "Well, we made a big decision here today. But quite frankly, I am excited to be in this adventure with all of you."

Ben sat Sophie on his knee and said, "Even you will be a big help. You can help your mother in the house and run after things for Jed and me. Each person, no matter what age, will be responsible in helping to make this all work out."

"What about the animals?" asked Rose.

"Well, we'll need all the horses to pull the wagons that far, "Ben replied. "The colts will follow their mother. The chickens we can put into their big travel crate and hang them under the wagon."

"What about Bessy, the cow?"

"We're going to give her to the Wilson boys. It would be too far for her. We got her from them, so she is going back home with them. We will have a lot of details to work out. Probably some questions we haven't thought about, but we'll deal with them as we go along."

Jenny spoke up. "We had better get our group home. The days will be going pretty fast and we need to be rested to make decisions about the days coming up. So long, Jed and Rose. Hope, come give Grandma a kiss."

Walking the family out to the wagon, they bid their farewells, each person going over in their heads the list of things that needed be done before they left.

Rose and Jed, with Hope standing between them, looked at each other.

Jed spoke, "Were we too hasty, Rose?"

"I don't think so. Things happened rather quickly didn't they, Jed? Just imagine seeing Aunt Laura and Uncle Thomas again! I never thought I would see any of my family again."

"It all seemed to make so much sense when the folks were here and explained everything. I hope that we weren't just caught up in the moment."

"No, Jed, I don't think so. It would have been much harder having them go and us staying here. Family is everything. We were happy here because of us becoming a family—Hope, you, and me. We are going to continue that no matter where we go or what we do. As long as we're together, there is nothing that we can't overcome because we are together."

"You're right. As Father says, it will be an adventure. We are going to be like Columbus and take a chance."

Rose laughed. "Even Columbus had doubts, but not as many as Queen Isabella did when he asked her for money and for ships."

"Thankfully, our journey will not be as detailed or dangerous. We don't need a ship, but we are going to need a wagon, and somehow I have got to figure out where from."

"Jed, I just thought of something! You remember my grandparents I used to go visit while my family was here?"

"Yes, why?"

"Their claim is still unsettled."

"And the point?"

"When they traveled here, they had a big lumber wagon. I think it may still be out to their homestead."

"Do you think so?"

"It wouldn't hurt to check. Let's ride out there tomorrow. We can put Hope in front of you on your horse. We'll take some bread and butter for a picnic. I can see the old place once more before I go. Wouldn't that be great?"

He had to smile at her enthusiasm. "Yes, we can check it out after chores in the morning. It would be good to know if there is a wagon available."

The three of them stood out on the porch. The sun was beginning to nod its head to start the long afternoon.

"This was a lovely home for us to start our life together, Jed."

He looked down at the beautiful auburn-haired woman standing next to him and nodded. "You are so right, Mrs. Carlson."

She grinned and said, "I really like that name, sir."

"Well, get used to it. You will have it for the rest of your life. We've got a big day in front of us yet. You go get me some dinner, and I'll take the horses to the creek."

"Hope and I are going to check for eggs. If the hens happen to lay some, I want to make sure we get them and not some wild animal."

With Hope skipping ahead of Rose, they walked into the coop, shading their eyes as they adjusted to the light. When they could see, Hope spotted the brown chicken chortling over her nest. She reached under the hen and was rewarded with a brown egg. Rose put the egg in her basket.

"Do you think that there are any more?"

There was one more hen on her nest. This time there were two eggs.

"Oh my!" exclaimed Hope. "She sat in the other hen's nest."

"That will make us a nice little supper, won't it, Hope? I have one more egg in the house, so Daddy can have two."

"Okay, I wanna help fix dinner."

"And so you shall!"

Chapter 7

Shortly after breakfast the next day, the three of them turned the horses toward the old homestead. Rose was surprised how run-down the place appeared. The house, even though Rose thought it was a nice house, had a run-down appearance. It was disappointing. The windows were broken, and the front steps were missing some boards. They stepped inside the front door and batted away cobwebs that graced the entrance. Only a few furniture items were still in the house. Rose stood and took it all in.

"You know, Jed, I just realized something."

"What's that?"

"The house makes it only a house, but the people make it a home. It always felt so warm and cozy when the grand folks were here. There was always a cookie in the cupboard and a fire to greet me on the cool days. But as I look at it now, it doesn't mean a thing without Grandma and Grandpa. It is just what it is. A building with no one or nor any love in it. I am glad I got to see it. This was really the only thing I hated to leave behind, and now I can do that."

"Are you disappointed, Rose?"

"A little, I guess. Grandparents are an extension of the childhood that we take for granted. We think that they will always be here. But in this case, it is okay. It would have been far worse to leave behind the old folks knowing that you wouldn't see them again. This way, I have the memories of this place, and I can leave knowing that while they were here, I could visit them. Does that make sense?"

"Yes, it does. It is kind of what we are going through. If the folks were to move to northern Iowa and we didn't, there would always be a big void for me. I would be happy with you and Hope and our new one on our homestead, but there would have always been something missing."

"I think that we made the right choice, Jed. Hopefully, Osage will be a land of promise, one that we can start over with and meet our obligations. We will just be starting a new chapter in our book. Fortunately, we have a lot of empty pages."

"You're right as usual, Rose."

"Let check the back of the old shed to see if we can see that wagon."

They looked around the place and finally found what they were looking for in the grove of trees directly behind the house.

"It's funny," mused Rose, "I remember that wagon being much bigger. I thought it held everything that the grand folks owned when they first came out here. Course, I was much younger."

"It looks as if it may need a little work." said Jed. "The wheels need some repair, and there are a few boards missing."

"Will it get us to Osage?"

"Sure, I'll work on it this week. It is not as if we are traveling across the country. Osage is only 190 miles. When we came out here, we could travel ten miles a days if the weather held up. We had to worry about bad roads, so at least we have the dry weather working in our favor. We should there within two to three weeks."

"Will we take the wagon home today?"

"No, I'll bring the team back tomorrow. It looks as if I had better bring the ax as well. There are a couple of little trees growing up through the bottom of the wagon."

"Will you need your father to help?"

"No, I think I can do it alone, but just in case, I should try to get an early start in the morning."

"How much stuff can we take along?"

"Well, I'll build up the sides so we can haul more of our belongings. The feather tics can go across the front, one on top of the other. That will save some room. We'll have the trunk for the clothes and the bedding. The box of dishes will fit under the driver's seat. The cook stove is not a full-sized one. I'm glad for that because we wouldn't have room for it."

"How about the table and chairs?"

"I think, but we'll have to put the table on its top and stack the chairs around it."

"Oh, Jed, the table is the only thing we got new. It will be all marked up."

"Maybe we can put a quilt under it to help protect it. It's about the best we can do."

"Can the chickens still be tied underneath the wagon?"

Jed got to his knees and looked. "I think so, but I have to make room for the plow. It might be quite a load, but I think the two work horses can pull it."

"Well, this should prove to be an adventure. I wonder how Hope will take it?"

"Probably better than all the rest of us. She can play with her doll on the bed and then just rest there when she's tired."

"Maybe some of the time we can have Sophie ride with us to help entertain her."

"That's a great idea! She will certainly fare better that the rest of us. You know, you may want to rest for some time too, Rose."

"Won't it be awfully hot in the wagon with no shade?"

"That's a thought! I'll see if I can figure out something like a piece of canvas to go over the top. It will protect our furnishings in case the weather gets bad."

"Jed, could you explain something to me?"

"What is it?"

"What if the weather turns next year and it does rain? We won't be any farther ahead up in Osage than we would be if we stayed in Lancaster. If fact, we'll be a lot farther behind."

"That's not exactly true. But it isn't just the weather that's the determining factor. The commerce of a bigger, more established city will bring a more promising future for us all. Sure, every area needs farmers, especially the men with businesses. They depend on the farmers to trade with them. The more trade, the more money they make. Farmers need a place to buy their seed and other things that they need to survive. It is better if that place is closer. We still have our independence on the homestead, but we are still close enough to the trading centers if we need anything."

"I see. I particularly like the part that your parents are going to be our neighbors and that Aunt Laura and Uncle Thomas will be close. They are an added bonus. I thought that I had lost all of that."

"Well, I know one thing. If we don't get moving, we won't be ready to leave next week. So we need to get cracking. Let's get those sandwiches and sit on the edge of the wagon with Hope. There are going to be a lot of long days in the two weeks."

Rose pulled out the box with sandwiches in it. "Guess, what? I brought along some cookies for a treat! No, Hope, the bread and butter first."

Jed started to laugh.

"What are you laughing at?"

"Do you remember the box socials that the school used to have when we first met?"

"Yes, I always made chicken and apple pie because they were your favorite."

"Right, I always made sure that I got your lunch box because I wanted to spend time with you."

"I remember. I also recall Henry, who was always trying to buy what I had made. He only did that a couple of times, then he quit trying."

Jed looked straight ahead, trying to hide his sly smile.

"Jed Carlson! What did you do?"

He let his eyes betray him. "Well, the second time Henry tried to outbid me, I was a dollar short, so I had to borrow it from my father."

"But why did he not try again another time?"

"Because I followed him to the outhouse and punched him in the nose and warned him to not bid on your lunches anymore."

Rose laughed. "And he told everyone that he hit his face on the privy door! Why, Jed, I do believe that you were fighting for me. How gallant!"

"Yes, and I didn't even know how hard I hit him until the next day. My right knuckle was pretty sore. But, boy, was that worth it!"

Rose looked at him and thought how lucky she was. A wonderful husband who allowed her sister to be a part of their lives and a new baby on the way, how happy she was!

They finished their lunch and walked a bit more around the farm. Checking behind the other buildings, there wasn't much else that was of use. Jed did find an old ax in the shed.

"It looks a bit rusty, but I think that I could scrape it off the rust so that it can be used again. Other than that, I don't see anything else, do you, Rose?" He looked around and didn't see her or Hope. "Rose?"

She appeared at the house door with a spoon in her hand. "Hope found this by the back porch. The grand folks must have eaten something out here and dropped it and forgotten to pick it up. I remember the set of silverware that she had. I wonder what happened to all of it?"

"It seemed to me that the storekeeper got to come out and pick up some articles that were of value. There was a few bills that hadn't been paid, so he came out to gather what he could to make up what he lost."

"That seems rather odd. I didn't know that they had any debt."

"I don't think it was much. Just for the seed and such. The storekeeper always has people owing him money."

"You're right. I forgot that Laura and Thomas always had customers that owed them. That's probably why the current owners left. The people just couldn't pay what they owed."

For a few minutes, Jed took Hope so that Rose could wander about the farm. She came back and nodded that she was ready to go.

"Up we go, Hope. Time to go. We've got a lot to do."

Hope ran, and Jed lifted her up and settled himself into place directly behind her.

Rose eyes followed the pair. Hope's body was totally blocked by Jed's. She smiled inwardly at how well the two of them got along. He was so big and rugged but became so soft and tender when he was with the two of them. Rose knew that many young women were not as happy as she was with Jed. Some women married their young men without having met them first. Some girls married men who were much older. There were marriages where the men were abusive. The women simply had to tolerate their circumstances as often there was no other place to go. She was in this place because that was where she wanted to be—a loving relationship where she was a partner and her opinion mattered. She had to thank Jenny and Ben for that. Ben was a rare man who trusted in his wife's thoughts, and working side by side with her provided for their family well.

Rose's mind had been busy on the way home. She noticed how tired the she was. She let Jed help her off her horse.

"Are you well, Rose?" Jed inquired.

"I'm just so tired. This baby is letting me know who it is in charge already. Do you need me to help with anything? I would like to take a nap with Hope."

"Go ahead. I've got plenty to do here. Supper can be later tonight. I'm going to fix up a crate for the chickens. It seems as if a tree branch fell on it and did some damage.

I think that I can salvage it. I forgot that I'll have to have a little space in the wagon for oats to last us on the trip. I have a feeling that we won't be able to take everything that we want to. I think the folks are taking two wagons."

"They are? Is your mother going to drive one?"

"No." Jed grinned. "Jake gets to take one. Freddy is going to ride with him. Jake is thinking that he is a man already. It is a responsibility, but he'll never learn any younger. We'll see how he does."

"Will they have any extra room in their wagons?"

"I doubt it. They've got more belongings because they have more people and have had a longer time to collect stuff."

"What about Sugar and the colts?"

"I'll tie her to the end of the wagon. The colts will follow her, so I shouldn't need to tie them. Go in and lie down, Rose. You look rather tired."

"I am. Come on, Hope. Let's take our naps."

Jed watched his girls go into the house. He led the horses to the disappearing pool and thought of all he needed to do before they could leave. He hoped that he didn't run out of time. Nor did he want his folks to have to help him. He wanted to sort and choose what he needed to take. He sat with his back leaning on the tree while the horses drank. It was hot, but the shade of the old tree helped to make it tolerable.

It was nearly an hour later when he woke up. "Whoa, this will never do! I am lazing away my precious time, and I've got work to do. I hope that Rose is resting."

He took the horses by the bridles and walked back to the pasture area. There, the two faithful work horses joined Sugar and the colts under the big cottonwood tree. The colts were lying down, trying to stay still and not let the heat bother them. Flies buzzed around the Sugar. She was glad to see the other horses. They would help keep the flies away by using their tails to keep the pesky insects away from each other's faces.

Even the chickens had problems. Little bugs were biting them. In an attempt to rid themselves of the bugs, they rolled on the dusty ground. And there was plenty of that. He recalled the first time that Hope had seen them rolling in the dirt. She tried that also and got dirty and got a lecture from Rose. Jed had laughed and said, "Rose, they all do that."

He spent the rest of the afternoon working on the chickens' crate. He was no carpenter, by any means, but he actually did a respectable job of repairing it. He admired his work and stood it up next to the stable away from the tree.

The ax from Rose's grand folks' homestead was next on his list. He filed off as much of the rusty edge that he could. It seemed to go deeper than he thought. It took more time than he wanted to spend on the project, but he was satisfied when he finished.

Noticing that the sun was not far from going down, he finished his nightly chores and locked up the animals for the night.

"Hmm," he mused, "I haven't seen Rose or Hope this whole afternoon." He walked up toward the house and looked in. He noticed that his supper was not getting fixed nor were the girls in the house. "Funny I didn't see them outside." He continued out the back door and saw Hope sitting by the outhouse. She looked up as Jed approached.

"Where's Mama?"

She pointed to the little building." She's in there. Her stomach hurts."

Jed pressed his ear to the door. "Rose, are you all right?"

"I'll be okay. I just slept so long this afternoon the baby thought it was morning and concluded it was time for me to get sick."

"Should we go to the doctor?" Jed worried.

"No." Rose opened the door. "Your mother said it was normal, morning sickness. It will pass before too long. Don't look so alarmed, Jed. It is all part of what I have to go through."

This having a baby was pretty complicated. Jed had never been around it. When his mother had his brothers and sisters, he got sent to the barn with his father. They worked out there for a long time. He did remember the time, though, when Sophie was born. She came so fast that the doctor couldn't get there on time. Benjamin had to deliver her.

Thinking about that, Jed panicked. "Rose, when the baby comes we'll have to get help. I can't help birth it."

She looked at him and wondered how his mind had gotten all the way from morning sickness to help to deliver their child in ten seconds. She thought to herself that men were sometimes strange. She said to herself, *It is not as if I can pick the time that this baby is born. I just hope Jenny will be around. She'll probably send Jed him to the stable.*

"Okay, Mama?"

"Yes, Hope, I'm okay. Let's go get some supper. Wash up, Jed. It won't take long."

So altogether they entered the house, each with thoughts of the baby and the events that would happen first before they got there.

Chapter 8

Now that the decision had been made, Jed felt a tremendous relief. He had put his heart and soul into this little place, and as he spent each day preparing for their trip, he realized what he was going to take with him was what truly important.

Fixing the lumber wagon was a bit more complex than he had imagined. It had been sitting out for a couple of years, so the elements of the weather took its toll on the rig. The entire floor of it was too weak to support all the things that Jed had anticipated fitting in. Replacing the boards and adding the sides to it was time consuming. Besides his other daily chores, Jed was busy from sunrise to sundown.

Rose was just as busy. She thought she would wash the heavy quilts but thought better of it. She was right. She might as well do the cleaning when they arrived in Osage. There were some things that couldn't be packed until the last minute. The bedding and the dishes would be needed for the last night. She would not use the stove on the day of the travel. It had to be cooled down before it could be loaded in the wagon. So the night before, there would be no fire, and it would stand clean of ashes and ready for the journey. She walked out to the wagon many times with Hope, eyeballing the space and whether it would all fit. Jed came up behind her on one of those times. Would it fit?

"I am hoping it will fit," said Jed, as if reading her mind.

"I have a few items such as the churn and pans and such. There should be little spaces here and there that I can fill up. I make have to pack a few rugs around them to help protect things."

"I have a couple of horse blankets that we could use during the day to pack valuables, but depending on the weather, I might need them at night."

Rose looked at Jed. "Really, Jed, I don't think that I want the smelly horses' blankets around my kitchen supplies."

"I thought that you might say that. But you may change your mind after we start out. This isn't a luxury trip. It will be pretty dusty, so everything will need to be cleaned when we get there. Your washtubs can be put into the wagon with the churn and pans packed inside them. I think that you'll be surprised with how much will actually fit in it."

"You can tie the buckets under the back gate. That's the where we put them when we came out west. We looked like gypsies, but it saved room in the wagon."

Jed laughed. "You know, I am kind of looking forward to this trip. We can't really take our time as we need to get the folks' shelter all ready and hopefully move into our own. It would be nice to have a place to call our own."

"I agree. It will be fun to stay with the aunt and uncle for a little while. There is so much to catch up on."

"I am going to ride over to the folks this afternoon. We need to set up a time and day in which to leave. Do you and Hope want to go along?"

Rose thought for a moment then said, "I have quite a bit to do, but I would love to see how your mother is managing everything. I know that Jake is driving the second wagon, but they have a lot of beds and more furnishings to take along than we do. I think that the responsibility will be good for Jake as well as Freddy."

"Freddy will feel as if he is on top of the world."

"I don't think that I want Hope in their wagon, but she and Sophie will be okay with your parents as well."

"I am a little concerned about you, Rose. Do you think it would be too much for you especially now with the baby coming?"

"Jed, you are such a dear, but having a baby doesn't release the responsibility I have to my family. I still have the two of you to take care of and all of the normal everyday chores. This trip will be an adventure for me as well. As your mother said, this was the best time to be going."

"Let's have a quick lunch. We'll take the wagon. I want Father to cast his eyes upon it and see if it passes his approval. I am sure it looks secure enough, but I want to make sure since Hope will be in the box."

"Okay, let's go to the house. I have a bit of rabbit stew from last night. I'll heat it up, and we'll have new bread with it. I just got a couple of loaves finished. We may have to get a few items such as flour and cornmeal for our trip."

During their meal, the conversation was continued.

"Father and I thought that we may have to catch our dinner as we go. Mother has plenty of supplies if she has the room for them. I am hoping that we can help her out with that."

"Goodness! There is a lot to think about when preparing a journey such as this. When my parents and I came to Lancaster, they did all the preparation. I just helped to load up the boxes. I never thought of where the food might come from on the trip. We did have our share of rabbit stew and prairie chicken though."

"Your trip was much longer. Didn't you travel from New York?"

"Yes, the terrain was more rugged too."

The simple meal was soon finished. Hope was anxious to see the grand folks and happily let Jed put her up on the wagon seat. The ground was hard and dusty, but Rose appeared to be happy as they traveled toward the elder Carlsons. Traveling by horse and wagon took a bit longer that riding on the horses, but Jed knew he needed to get the wagon checked out.

Hope slept in Rose's arms. Jed and Rose spoke softly as not to wake her up. When they passed by the dry creek bed, Rose lamented at the lack of water.

"Jed, how could this dry up so quickly? It was almost a rushing stream when I was here two and a half years ago."

"That's for sure. The last two winters were without hardly any precipitation. This year, there have been no rains to speak of. We are just in a dry area."

"Do you think Osage will be much better?"

"Osage is near the Cedar River. It has several small creeks that are off shoots from it. Yes, I think that we will fare better there. At least the town is large enough to have good trade. Father says the commerce is brisk from what he has heard. Your aunt and uncle appear to be doing well. I could find other work there if the farming doesn't seem to be successful."

Rose looked at Jed. "I never thought that I would hear you say that! I thought farming was in your blood."

"Yes, it is really. They say that what is bred in the bones comes out in the flesh."

"That's more like it! I can't imagine that you ever be anything different than what you are. But whatever you do, I will work hard with you to make sure that our living is a successful adventure."

"I know that you will. It may be tough at first, but we will have a wonderful life. Look, we're already here. Time goes fast traveling with you. Was it too much for you on this bumpy road?"

"No, it was fine. I did notice that you avoided the potholes. No, no problem. It was quite pleasant actually. Look, there they are! Sophie is coming to meet us. I'm glad that Hope slept most of the way. She'll be able to keep up with the other kids."

Jed stopped the wagon so Sophie could ride the rest of the way. Hope was delighted to see her. She adored Sophie, and Sophie loved having a little playmate that she could boss around.

When they pulled up to the stable, Ben greeted them. "Well, it seems as if you found a wagon."

"Hi, Ben. Is Jenny in the house?"

"She is. She'll be glad to see you."

Ben helped his daughter-in-law down, and Sophie and Hope clambered over the end gate and ran off to play. Rose walked up to the house and waved good-bye to the little girls who were so anxious to be together they hadn't even looked back at Rose. Entering the house, she found Jenny sorting through the cupboards and packing items in the crates.

Jenny said, "I have collected a lot during the past twenty years. I think that with careful placement, I can get almost all of it in the two wagons. Did you kids figure out what to use for a wagon cover?"

"Yes, Jed thought of that. He had a piece of canvas that we'll use to shade the wagon. Jenny, do you have any idea when we are leaving?" Rose replied.

"I think the day after tomorrow. Jake and Freddy have carried several crates into the wagon. We are leaving the front of the wagon open for sleeping. If we pile the beds, two on top of each other, then we'll have a sleeping place in both wagons."

"Jed seemed optimistic that our lumber wagon will hold everything that we will need for the trip and help us set up housekeeping when we have our own place again."

"Jed has a good eye like his father for things like that. Let's go out and see what the men are planning. Maybe they have an idea or two about the packing."

"Hello, you two." Jed smiled when he saw the two women coming out the door. "We were just visiting about the animals. The folks got rid of their cow yesterday and haven't been working the horses too much. Letting them get rested up for the trip."

"What did you think of the lumber wagon that Jed fixed up, Ben?" Rose asked. "It was on my grandparents homestead. It needed a bit of work."

"Yes, I noticed, Rose. I think it will get you to where we need to go. The wheels look sound. If there are any problems there are three good sized towns from here to there and a dozen small ones along the way that are bound to have a wheelwright. How are you kids looking for space? Can you get it all in?"

""Oh, yes," said Rose. "We don't have nearly the furniture that the two of you have. We are going to be pretty full, but we may have a bit of room here and there."

Sophie came up behind them. "As long as you have space for me!"

Rose agreed, and for the sanity of the rest of the group, the adults nodded agreement as well.

"I would suggest, Rose, that you bake up some hard tack for the journey. It really isn't the tastiest food, but it is something that we can pull out for a quick meal. I have my spider bake along."

"What is a spider bake, Grandma? Is it a real spider?"

"No, sweetie. It is called a spider bake because it looks like a spider, but it sets up on its legs to keep whatever is cooking out of the fire. I mostly use it for cornbread, Hope."

"Yum! I love your cornbread, Grandma!"

"So are we leaving for sure the day after tomorrow?" Rose asked. "If I know for sure I can get more things packed and lay out our traveling clothes. Your trunks are packed, Ben. If you pull the wagon up here, Jed can help you load the trunks."

Jed helped his father hook up the team to the wagon and pulled it up by the door of the house. The two men walked inside and tried to lift them up by the handles.

"Whoa! What do you have in here, Jenny!"

She laughed. "We've been in this place almost twenty years. It takes a lot of things to maintain a household. Do you want me to unpack some of it?"

"No." He called for Jake and Freddy. Neither boy was very big, but it did help to have them lift the trunks.

"I think that we should not put both trunks in one wagon. It might overload the horses."

With that, he drove the first wagon out of the way, and Jed hitched up the second wagon and drove it up by the door. The second one was not as heavy.

"Now, Jenny, decide where you want it because I'm not moving it again."

"How about placing it next to the bed but along the side? If we have to eat in the wagon, we can sit on the bed and the trunk."

"Splendid idea. Up we go, boys!"

With a heave and couple of grunts, the trunk was hoisted into place. Jed climbed up and dragged the heavy container into the center of the wagon into the place where Jenny had suggested.

"There, that is perfect!" said Jenny. "It will make our morning that we leave so much easier if most of the stuff is loaded. Is the plow going in as well?"

Ben answered, "Not unless there is room. Jed has room for his plow, so we're going to share it until I can get one.

We'll just have to do without some things until we can manage to buy what we need."

"This seems like a great accomplishment. Since we are going north on our travels, you kids can meet us in Lancaster on Wednesday. The earlier start we get, the better."

"We'll be on the road before daybreak. I'll have everything packed except for the beds and bedding. We'll keep the top bed made up so the little girls can play with their dolls or whatever. They can rest when they're tired."

"I think that we have thought it all through. If all goes well, we'll see you day after tomorrow."

Bidding each other good-bye Jed helped Rose into the wagon, and Ben threw Hope into Jed's arms.

"See you in two days, Grandpa," Hope said.

"That's a promise. And we always keep our promises."

With a wave, Rose and Jed turned back around and headed the horses home. Hope sat between Jed and Rose, who then found it nearly impossible for them to visit.

Jed looked over Hope's head, and he could tell that Rose was thinking about something quite serious. "I'm afraid that the days are going to be pretty long. You thought she would never talk, and now I am wondering if she'll ever be quiet."

Rose laughed. "Imagine what it would be like with two around."

Every once in a while, Jed forgot about that. But he was so happy that thought never stayed in his mind very long.

Before long, Hope was asleep on Rose's lap, and peace prevailed once more. Rose had to admit that she was tired. The distance to the folks was only four and a half miles. They would be traveling up to twenty miles a day. They would just have to stop and take breaks. That was all there was to it.

The weather was pleasant for the ride home. Rose dozed a little bit but woke up every time her head nodded. They were soon home, and Jed carried Hope into the house. She had been shoeless so Rose just washed off her pretty little face and left the room.

"I'm going to shut the horses up for the night and feed all the animals. Just fix a light supper and we'll go to bed early. We'll have a big day in front of us tomorrow putting the finishing touches on packing. You'll have some baking to do, and I have to get things ready for the animals' trip. They need more care than we do to get ready."

After they quickly finished up their chores, supper soon followed. The three of them were asleep before the sun went down for the night.

Chapter 9

THE NEXT DAY, Jed and Rose woke up to a day that was bright and fair. Even in the early morning hours, the sun beat down on the farm, encouraging the animals to seek the shade of the trees immediately after their feedings. Rose spent the morning with the baking of hard tack. She made several loaves of bread and packed the couple jars of jam that Jed's mother had given her from last year's supply. Jed spent the morning finishing up the collecting of the horse tack. He took the wooden barrel to the pond and filled it up as best that he could, thinking that the water would tie the horses over until they could get to fresh water from a stream or other water source. Both young people were busy all day putting the last-minute touches on the preparations for the trip.

Jed came into the house looking for a needed item.

Rose said, "Jed, I think that most of the dishes and kitchen supplies can be packed up after supper. I'll prepare supper earlier so that we can get the stove cooled down and load that up as well."

"I'll be ready shortly after supper. There are some things of the horses that I can't pack until I finish in the morning with their feedings. Either way, it won't take long," Jed assured.

"Jed, do you realize how quickly all this came up? I would have been content to stay here for the rest of my life. It was a perfect way to start our life together. But as soon as I heard that Aunt Laura and Uncle Thomas were still in Iowa, I was ready to pack up and leave. I think I am feeling this way because they are an extension of my own parents. But I don't understand one thing. We will have no money to make it through the winter. How are we going to make it?"

"Your uncle Thomas must have got to thinking about that. Remember Father saying that Uncle Thomas has had the claim for two years?"

"Yes, I remember."

"Well, if we can make it up there in time for the harvest, then whatever I can reap, Thomas and I will each receive half of whatever it produces. He has been farming that land, and there is a crop sitting on it right now."

"That is awfully generous of him. Why would he do that?"

"I think that he feels some responsibility as your father's brother. You were left with basically nothing, and they themselves have no children."

"Won't he need it himself?"

"I think that he and Laura have all that they can handle at the store. Osage has been good to them. He considers it a favor to him and Laura if we finish the three years left on the homestead. It is also hard for the two of them to live out there. According to the Homestead Act, they have to live on the claim for seven months out of the year."

"I didn't know that, or I forgot about that rule."

"Often at night, he has to travel into town and open up his store for supplies or a prescription that a doctor has given a patient after hours or during the night."

"In that case, I can see his reasoning. That would be rather inconvenient. Thomas looks so much like Papa that it may be hard to see him each day."

"I think that it will be good for you. Your father was a good man, and he was only in his early forties when he died. I think that you'll like being close to them. I know that they will like you being there."

"Yes, I suppose that you are right."

"I would have been content here as well, but since the folks were moving north, I wanted to go with them. It would have been hard not to see the kids again."

"So I guess that this is what we are supposed to do. It seems hard right now packing up our world, but I can't imagine doing anything else. I can hardly wait to see what our new home will look like. Hope is at a perfect age to travel. She'll adjust to a new surrounding."

"You're right. But to change the subject just a bit, there's a couple of your chickens that look as if they are a little lame. If we butcher them along the way, then they'll make a good meal."

"Yes, I was thinking that. We can make cornbread on your mother's spider bake and eat pretty well on the trip."

She came close to Jed and put her arms around his neck. "I am looking forward to all of this. I was sure, after Hope and I came on the stagecoach from the East, I was done with traveling. It will seem more like an adventure with the folks and our little family."

"Right you are." He kissed her on the forehead and said, "But now I had better get to work. The day will go by too soon, and I won't be ready for tomorrow. He hugged her back and turned to walk away.

"Come to the house for dinner in about an hour. We'll make both of our next meals early so we can pack while it is still daylight."

Nodding in agreement, Jed headed back to the animals, and Rose and Hope went back to the house. As soon as he reached the empty stable, Jed leaned against the center pole. Chewing on a piece of hay, he thought how hard he had worked for all of this. He had immersed himself into preparing it for Rose and for their life together. He felt that he was betraying himself a bit by being so anxious to leave. But he was leaving to go to an unknown place where his whole family would be. Rose would have family there, and family was everything. No, no regrets here. He felt as if he were a young boy again on the night before Christmas. He was ready to change his surroundings.

His eyes scanned the fields. All the crops had wilted. There was nothing there to save. The garden was all but gone. Maybe the rabbits could find a little food there. The well was dry, and the little pool in the creek bed had less and less water each day. No, it would have been a great place to raise a family, but Jed thought that moving to Osage was a good solution. The crops were dying here, the people were leaving, and Lancaster was slowly fading away. It was a chance for them all to start over. It would be a place of a new beginning, to be around family, and to be part of a new community. It was a place of promise, a place where they could settle down. In the early days of his father's life, Lancaster held promise. It was a promise of a place that would support a pioneer family. It was a place where help was next door with a neighbor. But Lancaster no longer held that promise.

As he stood there, his eye caught the lumber wagon. He noticed the space where their feet would be. Thinking that it might be better to have a bench for Rose to put her feet on, he looked around the farm. He didn't have time to build anything complicated, but it would be nice to have something there just the same.

He saw in the corner of the chicken coop a couple of hay bales that the chicken used for laying wayward eggs. That was exactly what he needed, and it would serve as food for the horses when they couldn't find anyplace to graze.

He grabbed the first bale and swung it up to his shoulder and carried it to the waiting wagon. After a bit of maneuvering, the bale fit into the foot space. He stood back content at his own idea. He took the second bale and placed that under where his feet would go. It seemed a bit too high for his long legs. As he tried to push it into place better, the bale broke and scattered on the floorboard. He found that to his liking and spread it around under the place where his feet would go, and it was no longer uncomfortable for him to sit there. That also gave him another idea. He went back to the stable and grabbed the last two bales that he owned. He spread them on the bottom of the rest of the wagon. That would serve as a protection for anything else being hauled. He felt that that was a job well done.

Rose busied herself in the house. Hope was helping her, so it was as if any progress made was soon undone. She had lugged in the washtubs and sitting them on the floor, packed the small glass butter churn and the few pots and pans that she had and some dishtowels. *There*, she thought, *now I needn't get into these tubs until we reach where we are going. But where should I put the items that I will need on our trip?*

She looked around the house, and checking the lean-to, she found a small wooden crate that she felt was perfect for the traveling dishes. She shoved it with her foot until she reached the kitchen cabinet. Carefully packing those items, she was happy that it all fit into that box.

"Hmm, what next?" saying that aloud more to herself than to Hope.

She knelt and looked into the pantry shelves. She saw an oval plate at the back space of the dish cupboard. It was a platter with a picture on it.

She read the painted words aloud, "Give us this day our daily bread." She put her hand over her mouth, and a muffled noise came out. "Jed, look what I found." She made quick steps out to the back of the stable where Jed was. He looked up at her as she came near him.

"Jed," she repeated, "look what I found!"

His smiled betrayed that he knew.

"Jed, this belonged to my grandmother. It was part of a set she and Grandfather got as a wedding present. It was the only piece that made it on their trip to Lancaster. How did it get here, and why didn't I see it before?"

"You didn't see it before because I found it the day we went to their homestead. I found it under the flour bin in the pantry."

"Why didn't you show me then?"

"I wanted you to be surprised, and it worked."

"What if we hadn't gone back there? It would have been lost forever."

"I say that it would have been worth the trip even it we had not found the lumber wagon."

Rose held it close to her. "This is really the only thing that I have that belonged to her. It is like finding a treasure!"

"I thought that you would like it. Hope actually found it. She was digging in the cupboard. I am surprised that you didn't see her bringing it to me. It is almost heavier than she is. I told her it was our little secret, and she sure kept it well. Do you like it?"

"I love it! Thank you so much! It is a wonderful surprise!"

Leaving Rose with her newfound treasure, he left the house promising to be back soon for the noon meal.

Rose carefully wiped the plate, thinking back on some memories that she had forgotten. She recalled the freshly baked breads that Grandma used to serve on that plate. Often a large baked chicken graced the plate for the holidays. No matter what had been on that plate, it was always a good reminder of the grandfolks. She quickly tied Hope to her chair and looked toward the building to see if Jed was on his way to the house. Dinner was ready.

As he was closing the stable door, he saw Rose in the doorway of the house. As he looked toward her, he smiled to himself and thought, *Rose is full of promise. With the new life growing in her, it is God's promise that the world should go on.*

He walked toward the house and joined Rose on the steps. She, too, was looking at the farm. There really wasn't any more to say. All of the words had been spoken, and they had come to an agreement on the outcome. Life was good as long as they were together.

Chapter 10

The final day on the farm started much earlier than normal. At four, the breakfast meal was over, and Jed was on his way out. Hitching up the horses, who even looked sleepy on this day, he drove the wagon up next to the kitchen door. Rose already had their bed covers folded and put away in the trunk. Jed wouldn't let Rose help lift it. He used a couple of boards as skids and pushed it up the ramp into the wagon. Together the two of them put the bottom of the bed into the front of the wagon.

"Now that is a close fit. Not one inch of room at either end of it. This makes it pretty snug."

"That's good," Rose responded. "That way, Hope won't fall out of it in case the roads are bumpy."

The box of dishes and the box of food were tucked under the seat. It was a tight fit, but there was still a little room at the back for Jed's plow. The underside of the wagon had several wires in order to hold the chickens' traveling coop during the ride.

Both Jed and Rose went out to gather the chickens still sleeping with their heads tucked. Most of them were taken by surprise, so they were loaded into the crate without much fuss. The last three, however, were very suspicious, so they were frantically running into each other and the walls before being captured by the two people. Jed placed the crate under the wagon and pulled on the wires as they lifted it into place. It did not appear as if the chickens were pleased, but they soon settled down for the ride.

Rose went back into the house, while Jed went to the stable. There was nothing left to pack with the exception of Hope's bed. But each adult needed the time to look over the area that had become so dear to them. Jed looked up in the loft of the stable knowing full well that there wasn't anything left up there. Rose checked the cupboards twice for anything that might have gotten overlooked. But nothing had been left behind that wasn't meant to be left. It was just each person's own moments with a place that helped them grow to manhood and womanhood.

Rose was happy to go because of her family. Jed was anxious because it meant a new beginning, a chance at a new start in a new place with those that he loved the best.

He saw Rose searching the farm for him, and he waved at her and joined her on the porch. "Well, this is the start of a new life. I must say that I am looking forward to it. It will be good to go to an area with good commerce and trade, don't you think?"

"Yes, I do. It is a bit surprising and sad at the same time, knowing how quickly we have sorted out our lives here. We made it so that any ties to the farm and the area are now gone and behind us. We can only look ahead and see what Osage brings."

"As pleasant as this is, it is almost five, and I'll bet the folks will beat us to Lancaster."

"I suppose that we have to get Hope up sometime. I'll go pick her up, and you can toss the bed in the wagon. I can dress her later when she wakes up. Hopefully, she'll sleep a couple of more hours."

"Don't count on it. She knows that she and Sophie will be spending time together. Once she figures out we're on our way, she'll be too excited to sleep."

Rose was successful in transferring Hope to her arms without waking the little girl. Jed carried out the bed and tried to make it up like Rose wanted.

"We don't have room for the trundle part of the bed, so we'll have to find something suitable when we get there."

Rose laid her sister on the bed in the wagon and took her seat beside Jed. Jed picked up the reins, and each cast a glance, surveying the farm. Jed turned to look at Sugar tied to the end of the wagon and the colts following her like baby puppies following their mother. Feeling satisfied that all was well, they led the team and wagon down the lane for the last time.

The sun was not in a hurry to get up. The day was going to be hot with no rain in sight. The canvas protected the sleeping girl from the hot sun. Jed had rolled up the sides of the covering in order to allow any breeze coming through to cool down the wagon.

"Jed, where is your gun?"

"It is under the hay behind my feet. I wanted it close in case we saw a rabbit or prairie chicken.'

"That's the only thing I didn't see you put in."

"I didn't want it to be back where Hope was riding. It is loaded, and if we hit a big bump, I didn't want it to go off. The safety is on, but I want to be careful."

They rode in silence until the little town of Lancaster was in sight. They had stopped at the stream where they used to skip stones. Pausing only briefly, they soon continued on.

"Isn't it funny, Jed, that I used to think about the time we spent here all the while I was back East? It was so important for me to be able to remember the places we used to spend time together. And now it is only a memory of the past, one that I will forever cherish, but I can look ahead for other opportunities to fill up my memory bank."

Jed didn't answer. He just nodded his head. As he continued to look around, he saw that his folks had just pulled into town. Jake was driving the second wagon, sitting high upon the seat with an air of importance. The horses knew how to drive themselves, but still, Jake felt like a man, even though he was only fourteen.

Stopping only briefly, the elder Carlson pulled his wagon into the lead position with Jake following and Jed and Rose closing in the rear of the group.

The town was still quiet in the early morning. Even the town seemed to know that another group of its citizens were pulling out. There was neither fanfare nor waving good-byes to old friends. Most of them were already gone.

Rose turned to her right side to see the two-story schoolhouse for the last time. "Remember, Jed? That's where we met and began our courtship. It seems as if it were so long ago."

Jed grinned. "You know, I almost didn't come in to the school program that night. My horses were tired after a long day, and so was I. I remember how beautiful you looked, and I was embarrassed because I was staring at you, but I couldn't help it. Thinking back, that's when I knew I had to see you again. You were the prettiest girl there."

Rose laughed. "I must admit I was quite taken with you as well. I could hardly recall my lines that I had worked so hard to recite."

"Yes, and the first time I walked you home from church, I was so nervous. Not that I was afraid of you or anything, but it seemed as if the whole town was watching. I wasn't actually well known for courting girls, and all of a sudden, everyone was interested in my love life."

Remembering Rose laughed. "Do you recall the time when you slept at the store with Jake? I was so frightened that he would die in the night."

"That was not my finest hour. Did you know that after you served me that huge breakfast, I took Jake to the folks and ate another big one? I thought that you would think there was something wrong with me. I ate it so slow. I wanted to be with you."

"I thought as much. I was almost late for school."

Jed thought for a second, then said, "Remember the singing school? That's when I met Henry for the first time. What a parasite he was!"

"Whatever happened to him?"

"His uncle was a banker in Sigourney. He went there to live and is quite successful, I hear."

"He is probably right where he belongs."

"He got married to the daughter of a cattle rancher. She is twice the size of Henry. I'll bet she rules the roost."

"Jedidiah! That's not nice!" She playfully pushed him on the arm.

"Well, she is!"

"Enough said. We have had a good time in Lancaster, but it is definitely time to find a new place."

The conversation stopped when they heard Hope in the back waking up from her slumber. Rose crawled onto the back with her and helped the little girl get dressed. She offered her a biscuit and helped her climb into the front with the two adults.

Hope was excited to be in the wagon and even more excited to see Sophie peeking out of Ben's wagon. "I want to ride with Sophie!"

"We will have Sophie ride with us the next time we stop the horses, probably at lunch." Then looking over Hope at Jed, she said, "That will give her something to look forward to."

He nodded.

The morning went by uneventfully. There was a small pool of water a few miles north of Lancaster. Ben pulled the horses to the water edge and let them drink. It was a very narrow stream, and they needed to cross it here. After his horses got their bellies full, Jake's team and then Jed's team took their turn. After each wagon was on the other side, it was time to get out, stretch, and rest the horses.

Jenny looked at Rose and said, "We may as well have our meal here. I'll get the salt pork frying, and if you made hard tack then we'll have ourselves dinner."

Ben, Jed, and Jake each took care of their team. Jake felt his responsibility fully and cared for his team as well as the two men. They tied the horses to small trees and let them graze under their shade.

The women soon had the small meal ready. Hope and Sophie ate fast so they could run and explore. Freddy was so glad to out of the wagon that he allowed the girls to chase him.

Rose checked the chickens under the wagon in their coop. "Well, they seem to be all right, but we'll have to think of someway to let them out overnight. I'm going to see if I can give them some water." She soon found a low pan and carefully placed it inside the flurry of feathers. "I don't know if they all got a drink, but they are at least better off than they were."

The noon meal passed quickly, and it was time to hitch up the horses and be on the way. Sophie and Hope quickly climbed into Rose and Jed's wagon and started playing with their dolls. The three drivers were soon ready, and the long afternoon in the hot sun began.

Chapter 11

The first week of September was probably not the most optimal time to start out on a road trip. The weather was hot, and it was all the horses could do to pull a load such as the one they were pulling and still make decent time. By the end of the second day, the travelers were in a routine and not much conversation between the wagons was necessary. Hope and Sophie were probably the best travelers as they had each other to stay entertained and they both had a place to rest regardless of whose wagon they were in. Jake felt his responsibility fully and kept his eyes on his horses and the road. Freddy, being younger than Jake, was more anxious to look around and wanted to walk for a while.

"No," said Jake, "you are to help me watch out for things that might slow us down."

"I am tired of sitting on this hard bench!" Freddy replied.

"Quit your griping! You're not the only one who has a sore behind. We've got to pay attention to where we are going. If we break an axle or have to replace a wheel, then that's another delay. So you've got to help me watch for big rocks or ruts in the road. That's all there is to it!"

Freddy turned his attention back to the drive and kept his eyes on the road. "Just the same, it would be fun to see if we can find something interesting along the empty creek banks. Since there is no water in them, it would easy to spot any Indian arrowheads."

Jake was not all business. He had grown up a lot, but a part of him was still a little boy. He was also anxious to get off of the hard bench and run around a bit as well. "You're right. When we park for the night, we'll have an hour of two after supper. Then we can check out the banks for anything interesting." As they stopped for the night, they decided that they had traveled about twenty-one miles in the two days.

"Not bad," offered Ben. "That still leaves about 170 miles. If we travel the same pace, then we should arrive in Osage in two and a half weeks. How are the little girls holding out back there?"

"Good," Rose replied," but I think a change of scenery would be nice. Would it be okay for them to travel in your wagon for a bit?"

"Certainly," said Jenny. "That would give you a chance to have a lie down. Perhaps we should do that every afternoon so you can rest up."

"I hate to give you all the responsibility, Jenny. But I do get weary from all of this heat and sitting up."

"Let's try it for a while. Chances are, the girls will sleep in the afternoon for a little while, anyway."

Rose checked out the chickens. They were tired of traveling in their rugged makeshift home. "Jed, look at the chickens. I think they need to get out a bit."

Ben came to look as well. "Yes, I suppose they even need a break. I have some chicken wire rolled up in my wagon. We'll just make up a circular pen that we can set up each night. That way, they'll get a little exercise and can search for insects themselves. How about if we have a couple of these chickens tonight? The two lame ones look a little worse for wear."

Rose looked and agreed with her father-in-law. "I think you're right. We might as well get some good out of them."

Ben looked for his youngest son. "Freddy," he called, "get the hatchet out from under my seat in the wagon. You need to butcher the two lame hens for supper."

While the three drivers took care of their horses for the night, Freddy got the hatchet and one of the lame chickens. Finding a stump, he quickly took care of the first butchering and gave it to his mother. She quickly scalded the bird, and Rose started to clean it.

Rose felt a little dizzy and had to sit down. "I don't think that I can do this, Jenny. It never bothered me before."

"Don't let that worry you. I'll have Mary help. You are going to find out that normal tasks will be more difficult to carry out during the early months of pregnancy."

"I would give almost anything for a bath. This weather is so hot, and we've had so little water that we just couldn't spare any for such a luxury as a bath. I can't wait to get into an area where there is a lot of water again. I know that seems selfish as everyone else is suffering too."

Jenny disappeared for a moment, bringing Jed back with her.

Jed said, "Rose, go lay down. You'll feel better. I'll bring a little water from the creek. You can freshen up a bit then lie down before supper."

"I think that I will. Thank you, Jed."

He helped her up into the wagon and went to get her the water.

After her sponge bath, she told everyone that she felt better. "I'll try not to sound so whiny. I just get so tired, that's all."

Jenny replied, "If it's any consolation, I was like that before each one of my children was born. It lasted about the first four months. It may be different for you, but you will get through it, I promise."

Hope heard that and piped up, "And we keep our promises don't we, Grandpa?

They all laughed. "Yes, we do. How long before that chicken is ready, Jenny?"

"Soon. So if you children want to explore a bit, do that now. I'll call you in half an hour."

That was all Jake and Freddy needed to hear. They raced off toward the little stream to see what they could find. Sophie and Hope headed for the wagon to sit on the bed and play with their dolls.

Jenny stopped them. "Wait, you two. You have a lot of time in those wagons every day. I want you to run off some of that energy while you can."

Off they skipped to find the boys who were trying to hide from the girls. They thought their adventures would be so much more exciting without the little girls. They walked further up the bank and followed the meandering stream.

"Look, Jake. See the rock I found? What kind is it?"

"Don't you remember the teacher showed us one at school? It is called a geode. If we break it open, then it will be all crystallized inside. Don't you remember that history lesson? They are all over Iowa. It was somehow cause by the heating and cooling of the earth to different temperatures."

"I don't remember that. I guess I was studying my own lesson when your class recited that one."

"More than likely, you weren't doing either one. You were probably daydreaming out the window."

They heard their mother call them to supper.

"Bet I can beat you!"

"Bet you can't!"

The boys raced off, and their father got after them for running around in the heat so. The little girls hadn't ventured nearly as far, so they were close by when they heard the call to supper.

The family sat on the wagon tongues and visited while they were eating the chicken and Jenny's delicious cornbread.

Jenny looked at her family, especially the boys. "You're gonna have to wash up a bit before bedtime. You'll rest better."

Freddy thought aloud, "I think that I rest better without clean ears."

"That may be," said Jenny. "But whether we are in a civilized place or not, you have to wash up before bed."

Ben added, "Since the hens are going to be in a fence tonight, you two boys will have to sleep out under the wagon. That way, if you hear anything getting after them, you can scare them off."

Freddy was delighted with the thought of sleeping under the wagon, But Jake not so much. "Oh, come on, Jake. It will be fun. We can watch the campfire and pretend we are cowboys."

That thought appealed to Jake, so they began to plan their overnight watch.

Jenny was concerned, "Is that really necessary, Ben. What if there are wild animals?"

"They'll be okay. They can sleep right under our wagon. I'll hear them for sure if they have any visitors."

Jenny was not sure, but she kept her thoughts to herself and worried a bit like any mother would. If her husband considered it was okay, then it must be.

Freddy showed his find to the others and explained how it got to be that shape. His mother was impressed that he knew that information. Freddy looked at Jake, hoping he wouldn't say anything. Jake kept quiet, and Freddy resolved to do the same for Jake someday.

Even though it was still warm, the campfire was a comfort to them all. It wasn't needed for heat, but it was pleasant to look at just the same. It was getting dark, so all of the parties went to their wagons to prepare for the night's sleep. The sides were rolled up in hopes of getting a breath of fresh air.

Sometime during the night, the fire was low, and Jake woke Freddy up. "Freddy, do you hear that? The horses are moving."

Freddy was sound asleep. "No," he answered sleepily, "I don't hear a thing."

Jake lays there a bit longer, holding his breath. "There it is again. Freddy, wake up!" He was jabbing his brother in the ribs.

"What is it?"

"I don't know, but whatever it is, the horses don't like it."

Ben and Jed were now up. "Does anyone see anything?"

Jake threw another stick on the fire. They were all looking out beyond the circle of the firelight. They could hear something moving.

Jed got his gun as he heard growling from outside the perimeter. As they were peering into the darkness, they heard the sounds of two animals fighting. They all listened and agreed it sounded like two coyotes. They were close to the wagons. Their growls were loud, waking Hope up from a sound sleep. Screaming, she went to Rose for comfort.

"It's okay, Hope. Grandpa and Daddy are out there. They are protecting us all."

In the flickering firelight, they all could see a coyote and a dog. Both were emancipated from their lack of food. Neither would have approached a fire, but hunger drove them to it, even though each animal had its own reason.

With a big yelp and a gurgling sound, the fight was over. The dog had killed the coyote and was exhausted from its' efforts.

"I think," Ben said, "that dog was protecting our chickens for us."

"How so?" Jed replied, "He might have been after them for himself."

"I have been watching him for the better part of the day. He has been keeping out of sight just beyond the last wagon. I have been leaving bits of food for him. When we stopped at noon, he wouldn't come close, so I left a bit of salt pork for him."

"He probably can't catch anything. It took all of his energy to kill that coyote. He was after the chickens for sure."

"I think that you are right, Jed. Let's leave a scrap of food for him. Maybe by morning he'll be gone."

Both Freddy and Jake wished for a dog. Their last dog died of old age, and they simply hadn't replaced him. They looked at each other and telegraphed their thoughts.

"Well," suggested Jenny, "we had better get some sleep. Morning will come fast."

On that piece of advice the family headed off to bed and fell asleep. All but the two boys.

"Jake," whispered Freddy, "I want a dog. We could sneak him in the wagon, and he could ride with us."

"I don't think the folks would go for that. They'd find out," answered Jake. "But maybe we could keep dropping food so he'll follow us."

"Oh, yes, that's a good idea."

"Not so loud, Freddy. Put some of your breakfast in your pocket tomorrow. We'll keep him interested in following us. Go to sleep."

And partly because Jake was the older brother and knew what to do and partly because Freddy was so tired that he did just that.

It seemed as if they had all just fallen asleep again when it was time to get up. Breakfast was in a hurry, and though the boys were starving, they tucked some bits of their breakfast into their pockets. Once the horses were hitched up for the day's travels, the women packed up everything that they had needed for the stop. Everyone climbed into their wagons and followed the lead of the head wagon.

Every once in a while, Jake and Freddy threw over bits of their salt pork for the dog, who they hoped was following them.

"I hope that the dog is still there," said Jake. "I'd hate to think that we were wasting the food. I'm hungry myself."

Freddy nodded his head in agreement. He kept looking back to see if he could see the dog.

Since their hunger was ever present, the morning seemed quite long. As they stopped to rest the horses, Freddy said, "I guess it might be about dinnertime."

Jenny laughed. "It's only about ten o'clock. We still have another two hours yet."

Even though they had traveled six miles thus far that morning, all the men agreed that it seemed later than it really was.

That night, because of the heat, the boys asked to sleep under the wagon. They used the heat as an excuse but were really wondering if the dog was still behind them.

They pulled out their bedrolls and threw another stick on the fire for light. Settling down, all were asleep within minutes—all but Jake and Freddy.

"Do you think he is still out there?"

Jake nodded. "Shh, we don't want to wake anybody up. You got any food from supper?"

Freddy pulled out a piece of rabbit that he had been eating. He shoved it in his pocket when his mother wasn't looking. He thought maybe his father had seen him do that, but he didn't say anything, so Freddy kept quiet.

The meat in Freddy's open palm was still there when Freddy and Jake fell asleep.

Both in deep slumber, the boys slept through the night with no interruptions. They woke up simultaneously the next morning, disappointed that the dog had not visited them.

"Jake, look! The rabbit is gone!"

Jake nodded. "The rabbit may be gone, but the dog is here. He's sleeping by our feet. Move slowly when you look."

Freddy was never slow about anything, but he was so wishing for the dog to be there he carefully turned and saw the dog watching the both of them. He was wagging his tail, making a perfect fan in the dust. He lifted his head as the boys sat up.

Freddy patted the ground beside his leg. "Come here, boy."

The dog slowly went to his side and sat next to the boy. As the boys were silently cheering the dog's actions, they could see the tall boots of Ben next to the wagon.

"Did you really think that after all the food you have given him he wouldn't adopt you?"

The two boys looked at each other, wondering how their father knew what they were doing.

"I was a kid once. Besides, I gave you the idea. I quit throwing out food because I knew you would start. No sense in all of us going hungry in order to feed a dog."

"Can we keep him?" Freddy begged.

"We'll try it and see if he can earn his keep. He has got to leave the chickens alone!"

Jake and Freddy cheered.

The pattern of travel continued for nearly a week. Water was still scarce and a bit slimy for the animals to drink, but it was improving. The dog, which they named Rover, was very good about scaring up an occasional rabbit. He generously dropped his hunt at Jenny's feet, knowing that he would be given something in return. He politely waited to be invited along when Jed or Ben took their rifle out when they needed to hunt for meat. They agreed that he was probably someone's pet and had fallen behind their wagon. Slowly, he began to gain weight and his fur began to shine.

Ben said, "We've been gone for ten days. I think that we are halfway there. Do you notice the tree line up ahead about ten miles? I think that we are closer to a more significant water source than we have ever been on this trip."

They all looked to where Ben was pointing. There was a difference in the trees. They appeared to be greener.

"I think that we'll be able to make it there tonight. We'll see if we are on the right track for fresh water."

Everyone was happy with that thought. Breakfast dishes were soon put away, and the horses were ready in record time. They were starting out with new energy and hope that this day would end up with expectations being fulfilled. Each had their own dream of what finding water would mean. Ben and Jed were thinking about the water for their animals. Rose was thinking about bathing in its coolness. The children were hopeful for a water fight. Jenny just wanted for each of her family members to get what they wished for. Fresh water would be a treat.

As they traveled along, Jed pointed out the crops to Rose. "Look, they are greener up here. In fact, they're turning color. I imagine, even though it looks rather thin, that they will be harvesting in less than two weeks. We'll have to keep pushing if we're going to make it in time for harvest."

Rose sat, thinking, *I need to not ask to stop and move around so much. We lose time that way.*

Jed was reading her thoughts. "You know, when we stop for you to stretch your legs, we aren't really stopping for long periods of time. We all need to move then too."

She smiled at him. "I know, but it seems as if I am only thinking about myself all the time. I'll try to do better."

"There is nothing to do better, Rose. We'll make it. If anything, it is the darn chickens that hold us up in the morning. Remember the day that Hope tried to help and she let all of the chickens out?"

Rose laughed. "It's funny now, but it didn't seem so amusing then. We all had to help catch them. Your father looked so funny when he hit a rock with his boot and went sprawling."

Jed laughed too. "Yes, but he was really determined to catch that hen. And he did!"

The noon meal was only a quick stop in order to rest the horses and to eat cold cornbread with molasses dripped on them. All were anxious to reach the line of trees to see what was there.

In the afternoon, Rose slept in the front of their wagon. Sophie and Hope were tired out as well, and they slept in Ben and Jenny's wagon. It was Rose who awoke and excitedly leaned up over the bed and said to Jed. "Do you notice the breeze? It comes right in the wagon! We must be getting closer to water.

"We are almost there. I was going to wake you up to see if you noticed the difference, but I thought it would be better to let you sleep."

Rose climbed beside him. "I feel better already. Oh look, how close we are to the trees! Can you see any water?"

"Not yet. Look at the green grass. The horses are going to be happy as well."

As if on cue, the horses moved faster of their own accord. They could sense the water and the coolness ahead.

Everyone was awake now, and all look expectantly toward the evening's goal.

As soon as the wagons stopped, each person jumped out and stood near the stream. The water looked inviting as all could see the movement of the current. The horses stood patiently while they were unhitched, each driver leading his own team to the edge. The horses drank fully. The colts frisked about, wanting only to play. The older horses knew they needed to quench their thirst. The women took off their shoes and waded in the water. The children were already barefoot. They went upstream so as not to disturb the horses and splashed and played as though they had never been in water before in their lives. It was as if the hot stench of the summer was slowly being cleared from their heads. The air was fresher, and moods were lifted. They all stayed where they were for a short time. Jenny and Rose were the first to get out of the stream. Ben and Jed took care of their horses and Jake's as well.

"He has taken this trip like a man, "said his father. "This once, I'll take care of his horse. He needs to be a boy for an hour or two."

After dinner, the women and the girls went down to the stream for a bath. They all played and shot water at each other. It was so good to wash their long hair and feel like females again. They dried with the towels they had brought down and dressed. When they returned to the camp, the men went down to wash themselves, not that they thought it was necessary, but their women folks said they should. Even the dog frisked about. Already he was a part of the family and felt loved.

As they sat around the fire that night, they all agreed that this had been a beautiful day. Their stomachs were full of prairie chicken and cornbread. They had washed the travels of the last two weeks off of their bodies and were looking forward to the end of their journey.

As they were sitting by the fire, a lone rider came up. "Howdy, wondered if I could share your fire tonight. My name is Williams, Edward Williams. I'm a surveyor heading toward home."

"You're welcome, friend. Where you been working?"

"Missouri. I finished up my work there, and I am heading back to my home."

They all looked at him with interest. He was a good-looking tall, lean young man about twenty-four years old. He had been in the sun a lot as he was very tan.

Jenny remembered her manners. "Have you eaten yet, Mr. Williams? I think there is some cornbread and some prairie chicken left. I'm not sure how much, but more than likely you'd have had if you had not stopped."

"I would be much obliged, ma'am. Whatever you could rustle up."

Jenny nodded for Mary to help her. Looking at Mary, she noticed that she was watching Mr. Williams with great interest. They quickly got back to the fire and sat as he ate his meal.

"My folks have a homestead about seventy miles north. My pop's been sickly, and my mother wants me to come home and take over the farm. I'm tired of traveling anyway, so that's where I'm heading. My folks don't have any other kids and they want me to settle down. My ma wants grandkids."

Jenny laughed. "I can understand that. Just where is home?

"Have you ever heard of Osage? It's the county seat in Mitchell County, Iowa. 'Bout seventy miles. I haven't been home for nearly three years. My seat's getting sore in the saddle, so to speak."

The family looked at one another. "You're not going to believe this," said Ben, "but that's where we're going to homestead."

"Small world, isn't it?" He looked at Mary as he said this.

Jed saw her blush and could hardly contain his smile. He remembered that look when he saw Rose for the first time. His sister was not much different than he was.

Ben spoke up. "Do you want to travel there with us? If would be nice to have someone who knew the territory ride along."

"I would be glad to, but please call me Edward." He looked at Mary, and she blushed again. It was a good thing that the darkness hid her face.

Chapter 12

The trip took on a new interest for Mary. She was intrigued with Edward and thought he was quite possibly one of the most handsome men she had ever seen. She was delighted when she heard he was not married and that he was going to Osage as well. Their talks around the fire continued after the others had gone to bed. The days went more quickly, and Mary was much more concerned about her looks than she was before. She had left a beau behind in Lancaster, and she felt that she had to give up the most when moving to Osage. Now it didn't seem like such a bad idea.

Edward proved to be a crack shot as he often bagged a rabbit or prairie chicken from his saddle. It was his way of contributing to the burden of adding him to their meal plan. He was witty and showed Jake and Freddy how he surveyed with the use of his instruments. They were fascinated with his knowledge, and often he rode with them in their wagon, with his horse tied behind. Each night, as they made their campfire for the evening, he filled them with stories and songs of his travels. He was clearly glad to be a part of their group as much as they were glad he was a part of theirs.

Each night, however, he insisted that he use his bedroll and slept by the fire. The only exception that he made was when the wind picked up and each person heard a sound that he or she hadn't heard for a while.

Jed sat straight up. "Rose, do you hear that?"

"What do you hear?"

"Listen! It's raining! It's hitting the canvas and running down the sides!"

They could hear Edward moving to the dry ground under Jake and Freddy's wagon.

Everyone was awake now, but no one made a sound. It was as if they were afraid the rain would go away if they said anything. The rest of the night, each person slept as they hadn't slept for quite a while. Rose placed her arms on top of the sheets so she could fully benefit from the coolness of the rain. Life was good.

Breakfast was done in a hurry. Everyone did their part, anxious to get closer to their destination. Even the chickens seemed more cooperative. Less time was spent rounding them up and putting them into the coop under the wagon each day. Each day, they were extremely dusty. They seemed to not mind. They got watered and fed each day and were safe at night from predators.

Each day, as Osage grew closer and closer, spirits ran higher and higher. Jake watered and fed his team. He brushed them until their coats shined. They all went to bed in their usual spots knowing that they were about to their destination. The only sound they heard all night was that of the dog barking once.

They woke up in the morning with the women working on breakfast and the men preparing to get their teams ready for the day.

Jake went ahead of the other two. Suddenly he yelled, "My horses! They're gone!"

Jed and Ben hurried to the picket line. The two horses were missing. The chains were in a pile by the trees. Ben went to pick them up.

"Did you lock them up last night?" Ben asked.

"I always lock them up, but I was in a hurry to eat, I must have forgotten to!"

Jed was angry. "Jake, good horsemen always take care of their horses better than they do themselves! You can't make mistakes like that!"

"Did anyone see anything last night?" Ben asked.

"Perhaps Edward did," Jake suggested.

They looked under the wagon. His bedroll was empty.

Freddy said, "I'll bet that he took the horses. He is probably a horse thief. Hanging too good for horse thieves."

"Oh, for Pete's sakes, Freddy," said Mary. "Don't jump to conclusions!"

"Mary," said Jed, "it doesn't look good. The horses are missing, and so is Edward."

"He wouldn't do that!" She turned on her heel and ran off to be by herself.

"We can't move without that team of horses. We might as well eat then figure out what we're going to do."

Over the morning meal, they discussed their options.

"I think that we should stop here," offered Sophie. "I'm tired of moving around, and I want a house of our own."

"Maybe we can use Sugar in place of one of the horses and try to lighten up the single horse's load."

"I don't want to use Sugar for such heavy work. She is not used to it. Besides, the colts follow her, and they would get in the wagon's way."

"You're right about that, Jed. They would get underfoot."

"How far are we from Osage, Ben?" asked Jenny.

"I would venture to say less than twenty miles. Why?"

"We can't certainly afford to buy horses from a farmer around here. Could we leave the wagon and come back for it?"

"We could, but everything would be gone when we get back."

Jed thought for a moment then said, "Maybe I could stay here with the wagon and have you come back for me with a team. It would take only three days or so."

"No," said Rose, "I don't like that idea. We need to stay together."

"Yes, but all for the lack of reasonable care, we are in this predicament."

"I know that it is my fault. I feel responsible. Freddy and I will stay with the wagon," Jake offered.

Ben thought before he spoke. "Jake, any one of us could have made that mistake. The important thing is I don't believe it will ever happen again. Your offer is a nice one, but no one gets left behind. We've already lost a good part of the day, so I suggest we look for some game and rest today. I may have to ride ahead on Sugar and go to Osage. Thomas will have a team of horses we could borrow. It's not a perfect option, but it may be the only one we have at this point. Let's see what tomorrow brings."

The day went by slowly, each person trying to stay busy. Most them were irritated at the fact that Edward—if that was his real name—had tricked them all. He had made friends with them and shared his stories and their meals just to get them to trust him. And they did. Jake was the one who trusted him the most

Jed kept busy with his horses. Rose and the girls spent time wading in the creek. They slapped patiently at the mosquitoes. Jenny straightened her wagon, and Mary brewed much of the time.

They all rested that afternoon. Even Ben and Jed took naps. Rose was glad that he wasn't thinking about the missing horses. The only one who didn't sleep was Jake. Even though he had not been whipped, he knew he should have been. He wished that he had been whipped. How could he have been so careless? He always had been so meticulous with the care for his horses. He didn't feel like a man anymore.

They ate supper around a quiet campfire. No one had much to offer in the way of a conversation. No more was said to Jake about the horses, but he felt beaten and sore inside.

It was getting close to dusk. With thoughts of turning in early, a sound of riders could be heard. Jed got his rifle from the wagon and said, "This time I'm going to be prepared."

The girls got into the wagons, and Jenny made Jake and Freddy come in too. Jake didn't like being treated like a little boy again.

As the sound got nearer, Ben said, "Jed, don't be hot headed. It may be friendly folks who can help out."

"That's what we thought when Edward rode into camp. We were all taken by him," Jed argued.

"Just don't start shooting and then ask questions. That's all I'm saying."

"I hear you. I hope I remember that."

Rover had been lying under the wagon. He made no movement to greet the stranger.

"Look at him, no barking. He seems to know that it isn't a stranger coming to camp. Come to think of it, I remember hearing him bark once last night."

Thinking back on last night, they all agreed they heard him bark once. What did that dog know that he was unable to tell them?

As the rider pulled into camp, they could see it was Edward. They all stared at him with a bewildered look.

"What?" he said.

Jed found his voice first. "Where have you been?"

"I went after the horses. What did you think I was doing? Didn't Freddy tell you?"

They all looked at Freddy. "Tell us what?" Ben voiced.

"I heard someone ride up last night. The dog was sharing my bedroll, and I snore so loudly that he probably didn't hear him ride up. Someone took the horses and got a head start on me."

"What does that have to do with Freddy?" Jed asked.

"I woke him up and told him I was going after the horses."

He swallowed hard and said, "I thought that was a dream."

"Freddy, look what worry you caused us? Especially me!" complained Jake.

"I'm sorry. I was so tired that I don't think I was really awake." Freddy hung his head.

Edward spoke, "You thought that I stole the horses?"

"Not me!" said Mary a little too loudly.

"How did you think I could do that after all you have done for me?"

"We're sorry, Edward. We jumped to conclusions without knowing all the facts. I hope you can forgive us."

He looked at them all. "I see how it looked when the horses and I were both gone. Apology accepted. Now, Jed, would you put down your rifle?"

Jed looked and saw that his gun was still pointed at Edward. "I owe you an apology as well."

The campfire was much friendlier that night. Edward told that he had a bit of good news for them.

"Osage is only eight miles. We can follow the river road instead of the stage road. It will save several miles. I forgot that it was still there."

They all lingered around the fire that night, and each person got into bed with a light heart and a happy thought that tomorrow would be their last day on the road—and a short one at that.

The next day, all were up early doing their part to make this last leg of their journey a good one. Breakfast was a hurried affair. The horses were watered, fed, and hitched up in record time. Everyone stopped and took a reflective look around them.

The crops around them were good. Corn and oats waved golden in the fields. It was harvest time. A lot of vegetation surrounded them. Animals and birds were abundant. So was the water in the streams and brooks. The buggy buyer was right. The crops were beautiful and the rains plentiful.

"Look at the sky." Freddy pointed. "See, this place will never be crowded. Look at all the empty space."

They all looked and agreed. The wagons were loaded again, and the families continued the last of their journey. Shortly after lunch, Edward stopped the little wagon train.

"Over the next rise is Osage," he said. "You will spot the general store very first thing."

As they drove over the small hill, they could indeed see the town. They were almost home. They already called it home. There was family, a new life, and the thought of a new promise—a promise that only Rose herself could offer. It was Rose's promise.